The Life Stone of Singing Bird

The Life Stone of Singing Bird

MELODY HENION STEVENSON

Faber and Faber
Boston · London

First published in the United States in 1996 by
Faber and Faber, Inc.,
53 Shore Road, Winchester, MA 01890.

Library of Congress Cataloging-in-Publication Data

Stevenson, Melody.
The life stone of singing bird : a novel / Melody Stevenson.
p. cm.
ISBN 0-571-19886-4
1. Frontier and pioneer life—Kansas—Fiction. 2. Indians of North America—Kansas—Fiction. 3. Mothers and sons—Kansas—Fiction. 4. Pioneer women—Kansas—Fiction. 5. Indian women—Kansas—Fiction. I. Title.
PS3569.T45644L54 1996
813'.54—dc20 95-25591
CIP

Jacket design by Jane Mjølsness

Printed in the United States of America

To my mothers,
my daughters,
my sisters,
and to
the men who stayed

Acknowledgments

I owe so many so much.

Thanks to Jack Lopez, for his free and freeing lead; to Cheryl Spector for her keen eye and unflagging support; to Dorothy Barresi, for her most generous encouragement; to John Clendenning, for getting me into academia; to Kate Haake, for getting me into this novel; to Jewell Rhodes, for her invaluable advice; to Lesley Johnstone, for her kind smile and gracious words; to Ben Saltman, for being everyone's hero; and to all the many other wonderful faculty, staff, colleagues and friends I've found at California State University, Northridge, who have influenced and informed my writing life.

Thanks to all of my friends, mentors, and supporters at the University (Oviatt) Library, including Sue Curzon, Clark Wong, Rita Linton, Sharon Eichten, Grace Shojinaga, Joan Burden, and so many others. Special thanks to Terri Ruddiman, whose unconditional admiration of all that I produce (children included) has inspired me in ways she'll never know.

And thanks, while I'm at it, to the wonderful Oviatt collection itself, for providing me with so much rich source material. I want to acknowledge a special debt to Henry F. Salkeld and Brewster A. Ruggles—two gentlemen I've never met—who lovingly covered and cared for their books on the Old West and who generously permitted same to be donated to the Oviatt book sale, thus allowing those pieces of their lives to fall into my hands. I hope that your fictionalized appearances in this novel will please you.

For their enthusiastic support, prodigious efforts, and practical guidance, I am deeply and forever indebted to my agents, Maureen and Eric Lasher. I am grateful to my editor, Valerie Cimino, for her kind assistance, and for giving me the opportunity to work with all of the friendly, helpful, talented people at Faber and Faber.

My family, of course. Could not have done it without you. Thanks to my good and patient parents, Laurie and Bob Dager; to my own personal daughters, Shawna and Sarah, who fill my life to bursting and who always make me smile; and to John, my most steadfast supporter and love.

PRIMARY CHARACTERS

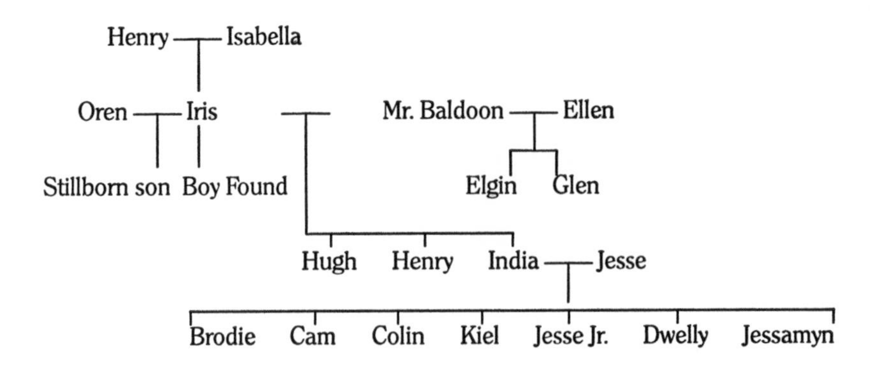

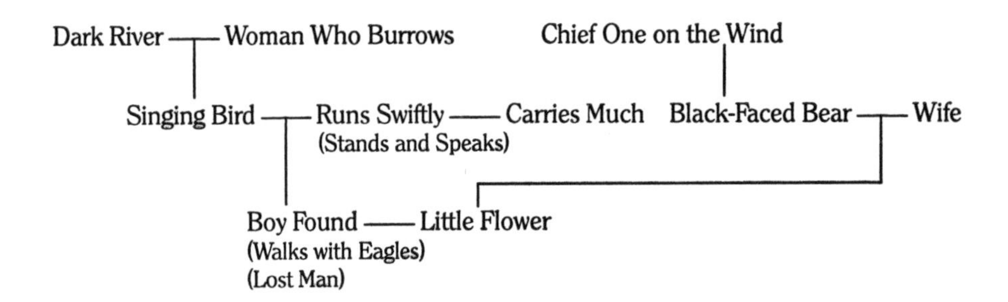

Contents

Prelude

Listen.

Ballads puddle up
in the cracks of your eyelids.

Mockingbirds nest
in the catch in your throat.

I am maimed and muted (like
her like him) but
my fingers are tipped
with those tender green swells
that precede the pink buds.

The sky has sucked up my borderless body
like silence
still
my need knows   no end

and my heart
beat still
echoes

FIND ME
HEAR ME
WRITE ME
Back in

to the wide open
s p a c e s

Artist,

can you carry me
inside
your violin?

Angel,

can you sing with me
a backward prayer (with
one wing flapping
against still borne air)?

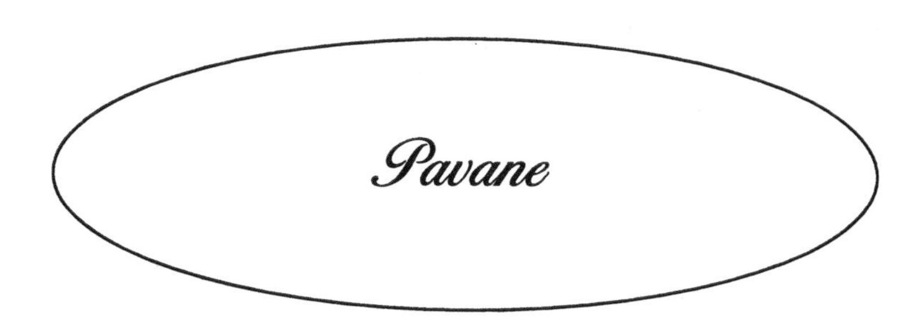

Pavane

After all those years of talk, of flying rumors, of mean excuses, of lies, in the end it didn't matter whether or not Singing Bird was invisible. No one saw her.

She crouched in the shadows of the sycamores, steeped in the fragrant tea of the morning forest. The rising dampness of sodden mosses and mushrooms clung to her trunk, her throat. Centuries of layers of dead wet leaves sank beneath her moccasins and gave up their steamy histories, rising like a smoke screen to shield her.

Six of them shouldered a great wooden box. The dark procession of bending figures trickled past Singing Bird like rolling tears. No one saw her. No icy fingers warmed near her ragged breaths. No crumpled hearts unfurled. Their eyes were dead, their ears were dead, and their slow shifting shapes did not even awaken the air.

Singing Bird traced with one bent finger the long welted scar that still divided her ancient face. The point of the knife had been inserted there, just below her right eye, and had been dragged firmly, righteously, across cheekbone, nose, and down, through perfect lips, so that a part of her smile would be left forever dangling.

"Daughter." Singing Bird dredged the word all the way up from her belly to her throat, but there it stumbled, bumped hard against the stub of her tongue, and then was swallowed in the low moan of the wind. No one heard her.

A girl child with yellow hair trailed behind the great box. From time to time she'd reach up and press a tender palm against a sharp corner, then stop to examine the round mark left in her flesh. She made soft sounds like raindrops falling on a lake. Singing Bird longed to draw the child near, to tell her of her mother, of her grandmother, of Lost Man, of the Life Stone. The child looked at the blackened, outstretched arm of Singing Bird but saw only another branch of sycamore. She did not stop.

The soft dropping sounds of the child's chant fell into a rhythm with her footsteps. Singing Bird glided through the shadows to follow, her coral bracelets tinkling delicately in the mist like fairy cymbals. The child stopped once, abruptly, and hit the box with her fist. The words she cried out were not in English. Singing Bird's heart rose at the words, with wings that strained to break through her brittle breast. But Singing Bird pressed her heart back inside with both hands and reminded herself that the child couldn't know. She was too young and no one would have told her. Certainly not India. No, the sounds the child made were only a few more soft splashes of innocent grief on the many pools of sorrow. And the Life Stone was gone.

So far I think it's lovely, don't you? Slow and stately as a bona fide pavane. A little too slow, perhaps. A little sappy. But real pretty and, except for the part about that poor old woman in the shadows, real believable. But you really should know, before you sink any more sympathy into that sad, abandoned creature, that she is my one true enemy. They call her Singing Bird, and her story is ground into my own like dirt in a wound and will be just as hard to get out.

But where to begin my own part in all this? I guess I should start at the ending, where the edges are sanded, the hinges are hung, and all that's left for you to do is turn the knob and step inside. Then you can feel it all whole, in one piece.

I'm already dead then, completely.

The good thing about my being dead is that I can see in so many directions at once. I can see past, present, future, mothers and daughters and sisters and men who stayed and men who left, and the crying, laughing, colors, contradictions, all butted up together, all on one big screen without edges without endings vast as the plains as the sky limitless. I can see my mother, giving birth to me, my father, small, already old, kissing her hand quick before he catches me as I slip out, Boy Found watching all of it. I can see my mother's mother at her daughter's wedding, smiling victoriously, dry-eyed, while my mother's father, silent in the pew, weeps with fear and rage.

The other good thing—the only other good thing far as I can figure—is that now I can show it all to you. And you can make it matter.

I am the one in the great wooden box. I am India. But you must know that much already. Except that I'm not really there. There's no life in that box. No space. No color.

The man you see walking, the one behind the little girl, is, was my husband, Jesse. He is a good man, and strong in his own way, though you see him stooped there and dragging his feet through the mud. He loved me. That's the part I want you to see first. But not just yet.

The two men carrying the front of the coffin (both are wearing dark brown homespun coats, so that won't help you tell one from the other) are my sons, Brodie and Cam, the only two left of six. They are still boys, really, sixteen and eighteen, but they are tall like men, and dark like their father, and flawed, and proud. The other four are all gone, thanks to Singing Bird. She breathed a fever into Colin and Kiel, sent a snake after Jesse Jr., and Dwelly she changed into a little yellow bird, to keep her company I guess (since her own son refused to) up there in all that blue.

In the center are my brothers, Hugh and Henry, and the two men carrying the rear of the coffin are neighbors. The older man used to be friends with my father. His name is Stewey. He was the one my father punched at my mother's boarding house. That was long before I was born, but if it hadn't happened I might not have been. Stewey and my father were still friends after that, or at least Stewey thought so. My father didn't forget much. Stewey turned out to be okay, though. He brought my mother a bouquet of blue lupine and a side of salted bison later on, after my father died. And he was the only one who put his arm around me at Dwelly's funeral. I don't forget much either.

Stewey's getting old now. He's really too old to be carrying so much. See, I knew it, he stumbled. Cold beads of sweat pop out on the thin, freckled skin of his forehead, and he struggles to get that box back up on his bony shoulder. My husband runs to help. I knew he'd do that too. He smiles at Stewey and shoulders the burden himself. I'm glad. It will make him feel better.

That little girl—the child that Singing Bird is itching to get her claws into—is my daughter, my baby. Seeing her like that, alone, bewildered, knowing that it is my death, my fault, that she must press her tender palm into the sharp corner of her mother's coffin in order to bring back some part of her living world, if only the painful part, cuts me, drags like a knife through my soul. It isn't fair. Singing Bird got off easy compared to me; only her face was disfigured. My soul is scarred and dangling, and yet I am powerless still, in death as in life.

Worse, because now you are the only one who can hear me. You, who do not love me, and whom I do not love. Worse, because now I will always hear my daughter's cries, always know that now she is deaf to my words of comfort. She thinks I have left her alone.

My daughter is blonde like I was, and pretty. Not that I am pretty now, though I could have been if I'd cared to be. Fact is, when you die you get your choice of resting in any of your living bodies, or none of them. The young and pretty one is not the one I chose. For a while there I preferred my worn and comfortable body. The one I had just before that thing started growing in my lungs and eating up my breath. Men talked to me in that body, about the price of wheat and about their dried-up wells. And they listened to me too. And their wives started giving me their softened eyes and their recipes for berry pudding and scalloped apples instead of the rustle of their stiff, starched skirts. Young and pretty was something I let go of with as much relief as regret. I gave up some power with the beauty, I'll confess, but that power was never one I could rest against. It opened doors I wanted shut and it blinded the very people I most desperately needed to see me.

But now it appears that I've wiggled out of my flesh altogether, so none of that matters anymore.

My daughter is smarter than I was, but she is not, I must tell you, any wiser. I can see her future filled with reds and purples and blues and yellows, just as mine was. She will love richly and miserably. Her life will fill up and up until it overflows into death. And she will find the Life Stone of Singing Bird. Even though I've done every single thing I could think of since the day she was born to keep that from happening.

Ballades

My own mother, Iris, married for love. That was why my grandfather wept at her wedding. He knew how love weakened, consumed the self, muted the voice. He knew because, loving Isabella, he had been weakened, consumed. His own voice was now so muted that he could do nothing but weep quietly in his pew. With fear for his daughter. And rage.

My grandmother, however, did not believe for a moment that Iris married for love. That was why, during the wedding march, Isabella was able to smile the smile of one who knows better. Iris wanted to escape, that was all. Just as she had, at her age. It was history repeating itself. And although Isabella would sorely miss her firstborn daughter when she left, she understood her need to fly away, to leap onto the back of a well-heeled, well-muscled young man who would carry her far away, to a place where she could escape her childhood, her neighbor's expectations, the stultifying air of respectable captivity. Isn't that what Isabella had herself accomplished? And hadn't it turned out rather well? My grandfather had happened along at just the right moment. He was a rich, propertied young American traveling in France, sent there by his parents to flaunt their wealth in the faces of the Europeans.

Henry had been crushing golden leaves with his heavy boots on a gloomy side street in Paris when he saw her. It was twilight, and he was wandering, lost in hard-won melancholy, savoring his romantic illusion of moving with neither will nor direction. Isabella was sixteen, panting and flushed from tearing down the broken sidewalk after her little brother. Her black curls were bouncing damp about her face and falling, falling like the Roman Empire, Henry thought, and instantly, forever for Henry, Isabella embodied the forbidden, the faraway, his first burning sip of Bordeaux wine, the perfume of the Seine, the purpose of his suffering, the object of his quest: his beloved.

Later, when Isabella was telling her girlfriends about it, she remembered Henry's strong, aquiline profile, and the gentleness of his gaze, and the tender quiver of his touch when he raised her fingers to his lips, but just then, to be frank, she saw only the trim cut of his waistcoat and the fine leather of his boots. She saw a man who was taller than she and who probably would not hurt her, and who just might be strong enough and needy enough to lift her out from under the suffocating blanket of tradition and predetermined fates and up into a world where mornings were fresh with possibilities, where the air, American air, was still new enough to breathe.

When Isabella ran home and told her mother that she was going to marry an American and sail away, her mother was not understanding. She locked her in her room, in fact, forcing an elopement, forcing Isabella to mourn her mother even while she lived, forcing Isabella to relive the tender moment of parting that should have but never did precede her journey over and over again, until little lines of regret and bitterness settled around her mouth. I will never do that to my daughter, Isabella vowed. I will understand.

But Isabella did not understand; Iris really did marry for love. And Iris did not want to leave her home, her family. She loved Virginia, loved the plantation her father had given her mother as a wedding gift. She loved the smell of the sweet alyssum and she loved the long summer afternoons spent under the shade of the live oaks chatting with her sisters, and with the young men who came by with their fists full of violets. Those slender young men were pretty and pleasant and harmless.

Except Oren. He was different. His family came from New York and had only just relocated in Virginia to pacify his mother after her breakdown. He was slender and pretty like the others, but instead of lingering in the shade, instead of resting at her feet and fingering the satin of her hem, Oren was always in a hurry, as if there were something very important he had to do before it was too late. He'd sweep by and drop a bundle of books in her lap, usually muttering something like "You must read these" before he rushed off again. The other young men would laugh when he left, or sometimes cluck over his intolerable manners, but Iris never laughed. The books felt heavy in her lap, foreboding. Sometimes she'd flip through a volume of Keats or Shakespeare and blush to imagine what Oren was trying to say. Other times she'd brush them like spiders off her skirts, roughly, angrily, without even glancing at the titles, so frightened was Iris that her future might be written within.

On one cold and sunny afternoon, too cold and too bright for pale sisters and earnest young suitors to accompany her outdoors, Iris sat alone in the lengthening shadows and shuddered. Oren. She felt him before she saw him, and when she saw him she looked away. How long he had been standing there, watching her, fitting his own long shadow into the shadows of the willows, she did not know. She closed her eyes as he approached, turned her face to the sun, focused on the orange and russet shapes that danced and flickered behind her eyelids, knowing what she would see if she looked at him, knowing what she would hear, knowing that that would be it. The end.

Oren stood still over her like that, more shadow than man, when he asked her. Without kneeling, without fingering her hem, without looking in her eyes, even, for she kept them closed. Iris said she would. She would marry him. She would go with him. She would be his wife and she would love him forever. And when he left she wept, like her father, with fear and rage, because it was all true.

When my mother gave me the Life Stone, years later, she wept again. But she was a different woman then. She walked with me far into the corn fields, where no one else could find us. She looked all around, suspicious, alert, though there was plainly nothing to see but cornstalks, tall and green and boring as always, and it irritated me, I remember, the way she was acting, as if even the lizards might be interested in what she had to say.

Iris was a different woman. She had long before made peace with her fear and her rage. She had learned to welcome and embrace them. They were old enemies who had done their best to destroy her and failed. Now she invited them into her kitchen and poured them a cup of hot chamomile out of her copper kettle; she listened to their impotent boasts of future conquests with tolerance, pity, and a certain condescension.

Oren's death had been only the first step of many in the transformation of Iris. For a long time she blamed herself for his death. She thought (I can see now, though I never guessed it while I lived) that she had called for it, attracted it somehow, just by fearing it so compulsively. She imagined that the force of her premonition, the paralyzing weight of the dread she could not expel, the noise it made when it knocked around in her body, drew tragedy same as blood drew vultures.

Oren died of idealism, but an arrow in his temple was the more immediate cause. He had been reading Rousseau that morning, early, by the light of a kerosene lamp. He had awakened Iris to tell her about the Noble Savages they were bound to meet. His voice grew deep and rapturous, filling their small wagon with tales of purity and goodness, of serene, uncalculated love for the world and everything in it. Iris, already heavily pregnant and exhausted, kissed her husband on the arm because that was the part of him closest to her mouth, then turned over and went back to sleep. She dreamt, as he spoke, of a long narrow river, roaring with the rush of new rain, biting off chunks of earth as it sped past, swallowing every bank in its path, churning them into mud, carrying them away.

When she awoke, he was gone. She fried dough in fresh suet but could not eat. The wagon train prepared to move on. After a time she realized that she must climb back up on the wagon and drive the team herself, or she and Oren's unborn child would be left behind. She didn't cry or tell anyone of Oren's absence, fearing that the sounds of worry might make real their cause.

The caravan had stopped again, for supper and sleep, before Oren's old bay found her wagon. Oren was slumped over its neck, the arrow still lodged in his skull. My mother didn't scream, just tugged and tugged until she got it out, with small chips of bone caught on the barbs. She stuffed the hem of her skirt into the hole, halfheartedly, knowing that she couldn't keep the life from leaking out, knowing that she had always known it would. She tried to lift him off the horse, but succeeded only in pulling him down into the dust, on top of her. That was when she cried, to have gotten dust all over him like that. And that was when the others came running. Three women caught a glimpse of Oren's bloodless, dusty face, then hurried their children away from the sight. Two others cried bitterly, dejectedly, for they were cold and filthy and nothing had turned out to be what they'd expected and this on top of everything else was more than they could bear. Four men hefted Oren into the back of my mother's wagon.

"Goddamned cutthroats," one of them said. "They're gonna pay, little missy, don't you worry." The wagon master told her that they'd have to wait until morning for the burial as the light was already shot.

Singing Bird arose with the sun. As a small child she awoke always with a smile and wandered around camp chirping little morning tunes outside of each tipi until the tall people stirred. The Men Among Men were generally indulgent with their children, and viewed idiosyncratic behavior as evidence of a smiling god. They did not, therefore, chide Singing Bird for disturbing their rest, but tolerated her morning visits. At least at first.

The tall people did not know that the reason Singing Bird sang at the flaps of their tipis was because new days frightened her. Singing Bird never knew what might happen and wanted some company with her when it did. Sometimes the clouds would turn black and rumble and shoot great spears down at Singing Bird and her mother. Other times the chief, One on the Wind, would send all the boys away, and when they came back they were bleeding and different. Now and then the tall people would paint their faces and chant and dance, and that was wonderful. But it could also happen that another tribe might come and steal away little children like herself and club their fathers to death.

She sang a special song for the chief, for he was powerful and good, and for this consideration he honored her with the name of Singing Bird. He called her his special child and instructed her mother to stitch coral beads into all of her garments, and to paint golden orbs always on her cheeks. He instructed the people of the tribe to arise when they heard her and to welcome her songs, for she was the guardian of the morning.

As the years passed she continued her morning ritual, and her people continued to tolerate it as instructed. But as her desperate need for companionship waned, so did her enthusiasm for the task. Her limbs lengthened, her voice deepened, and some of the boys who had come back bleeding and different glared at her as she passed. She wished she did not have to pass the tipis so early in the morning because sometimes those boys would hide in the darkness then jump out at her with a shriek. That made it difficult for her people to welcome her dawn arrival, and after a while they began to blame her for the disturbance, covertly, with frowns and sideways glances, rather than blaming the boys, now regarded as young braves and beyond reproach.

She cried to her mother to speak with Chief One on the Wind, but her mother continued to stitch coral beads into her garments and to paint golden orbs on her cheeks and she yanked her hair, as she braided it, every time Singing Bird spoke of the matter. Singing Bird knew better than to go to her father. Her father, Dark River, had more coups to his credit than any other man in camp and felt acutely the responsibilities of his rank. The skin on his face was stretched tight, like the scraped hide on his warrior shield. There was no elasticity to it, no surplus. Singing Bird feared that any extra strain placed on that skin, as that made by laughing, or by worrying, or by scowling to understand, might make it split apart at its invisible seams.

Well, I confess I have my blind spots where Singing Bird and truth are connected, and I suppose that might have been what her early years were like, but still, I sure would like to know why she chose me, why she needed me to suffer with her for her sins, why she made me do the things she did.

Used to be I saw her everywhere, all the time. She hovered so I thought sometimes I just might lose my mind. But in the beginning, at least, she was no more to me than a horned toad in the dust—ugly as all get out, but easy enough to ignore.

I was eighteen years old and real close to being married off the day I walked into the corn fields with my mother. The oldest Bean boy (that was their name, can you imagine?) had been hanging around for months, kicking up dust, telling my mother that she looked mighty pretty, helping my father get rid of our rats. He was okay, really. He had a shy smile, and I liked the way he stumbled over things—rakes, rocks, hogs—whenever he looked at me. But I didn't love the boy, and when I told my mother that she looked relieved. She told my father, I guess, because I saw him put his arm around the Bean boy one sunny morning and say in his Scottish brogue, "You air a fine lad, my son, but you'd best be fishing where they'll be taking the hook."

Then came the others. Plump, soft boys with overbites, big boys with dirty fingernails who sweated too much, rich boys whose fathers owned the general store or the *Tribune* but who just could not kiss, and one by one, my father took them each aside while my mother watched from the porch and rubbed her hands up and down her muslin skirts.

One scorching midday, my father having just come in for supper, and we all of us just nibbling on our dry cornbread and staring out at the empty sky, we saw a huge herd of longhorn go stomping right through our corn fields. My father saw it first; he ran for his shotgun and started shooting. Right away then we saw the cowboys wake up and start riding like their lives depended on it, which they did. After a while my father stopped shooting and the cattle started to calm down and the cowboys were able to get them herded a bit, way out on the edge of our field, so far out that they looked more like a thundercloud gathering than a herd. Then two of the cowboys came galloping back to my father.

My father kept his shotgun lifted, and I noticed that when they saw that double barrel aimed at their eyebrows, they took off their hats and kind of raised up their hands as they rode. The heavyset one shouted, "Sorry, mister," and they slowed their horses to almost a walk. When they reached my father's porch they explained that it had been a mistake, that they had been on the trail for weeks, and that all the men were so worn out that they must have drowsed off in the hot sun. They were powerful, powerful sorry, the one man kept saying.

The other man, the one who didn't talk, was taller and skinnier and, I noticed, a whole lot younger. He smiled at me while he dusted the corn silk off his thighs and asked me real quietly, while his friend was still apologizing and while my father was still spitting Celtic curses, if he could trouble me for a drink from our well.

I saw my mother roll her eyes before she retreated into the cabin. I stepped off the porch and felt the boy watching me walk. Then I heard his boots clunk down right behind me, treading hard on each flat stone just as I'd stepped off it and I had to stop myself from turning around altogether. I pulled up the bucket and plunged the metal dipper deep; I filled it so full that the water ran down my arms when I handed it to him. He said something to me about my hair looking like sunshine, or maybe he didn't, but I heard something like that and it made me glad I had taken my friend Callie's advice and rinsed it with lemon juice that very morning. The way that cowboy looked at me as he took the water, and this part I know for sure happened, made my hand shake so much that I guess my father saw it all the way from the porch, because then he hollered at me not to be sloshing our good water all over the feet of those blamed itinerants.

I followed my mother around for days afterward, recounting every little detail about that cowboy. His hair was dark and straight and greasy, like an Indian's. He wore a grimy blue handkerchief knotted around his throat. His skin was brown as fresh coffee, and did she notice how that long, hard muscle in his right arm bunched up and pushed out from under his rolled sleeve when he lifted that metal cup to his lips? My mother's smile grew a little sadder with each telling, until one day she took hold of my elbow, kissed my father good-bye, and walked with me far into the corn fields.

As I started to say before, Iris was acting strangely in that corn field, wary and suspicious. I kept asking her what she was looking for, squinting her eyes to see farther, deeper into the stupid corn.

"Nothing," she said, but her glance kept darting around while she spoke. "I have something to give you," she said, unbuttoning the top buttons of her blouse and reaching deep inside. She pulled it up in her fist and kept her closed fist before my eyes. "This," she started to say, but I interrupted her and pointed to Gonner's Cliff.

"There she is again," I said. My mother whirled to her left; her weepy eyes dried up real quick, but she kept her fist clenched.

"Who is it?" she asked.

I didn't have any idea. But I saw her all the time, standing always far enough away to ignore, watching me.

"Is she an Indian," my mother asked me, "with long black braids?"

"More like gray," I told her.

"Her face is disfigured?"

"Really ugly," I said.

She turned back to me then. "I can't see her anymore," she said sadly, though I still can't understand why that would have made her sad. "It must be your turn now." Slowly she opened her fist, palm upward, to reveal a plain brown stone attached to a coarse steel chain. She unclasped the chain from around her neck. "Daughter," she said as she reclasped it around mine, "I am giving you the sacred stone. Wear it always, as I have."

I tried to appear excited, for her sake, but I hadn't eaten in hours and was suddenly anxious to get out of that buggy corn field and into a plateful of black-eyed peas. "I just love it," I told her, and touched the brown stone for emphasis. Then suddenly, strangely, I began to tremble. My teeth chattered and I clutched at my own arms to stop the shaking. My mother pointed to the stone. It was glowing gold and leaping like a tethered cat on my breast.

Oren's only son was stillborn. Iris wrapped him up in the tiny silk blanket that Isabella had stuffed in with her china. She pressed the lifeless bundle to her breast and rocked him all night, hunched over on the floor of the wagon. In the morning, Hattie Linke found them and tried, with tears and whispers, to take the baby away. "He's in God's hands now," she said, but Iris kept rocking. Hattie ran and found Eula Blankenship and Dollie Moss, but despite their collective pleading and reasoning, Iris just kept shaking her head. Iris detained the wagon train for over a day and a half, until patience and sympathy wore thin and finally the wagon master declared that she was plumb loco and that it might be better to move on without her.

Hattie feared for her friend. When Iris finally fell asleep, she silently, stealthily removed the infant from his mother's arms. She buried it quietly under an elm, said a hurried and apologetic prayer, hopped onto Iris's wagon herself, and motioned to the wagon master to move on. They weren't a mile out when the jostling of the wagon woke Iris, and her low sobs dug into Hattie's heart. "Don't you worry, hon," she called back to Iris once. "He's with his papa now." But the sobs continued and they stuck in Hattie's throat, and although she repeated to herself, "I done the right thing, I done the right thing," until the words rose and fell like a hymn, Hattie clung to her own children that evening at dinner as if their small spirits might fly right out of their frail bodies if her own large, warm, substantial self wasn't firm against them every second.

That night the dark river kept rushing by, biting off chunks of earth. The earth screamed and cried to Iris, "See? See?" But Iris couldn't see. She couldn't open her eyes and she couldn't move her legs. Still the earth screamed and cried to her. Cried like a starving infant, desperately, hopelessly, hoarse from crying. Her hard breasts gushed milk and the cold wetness of her nightdress woke her. Iris opened her eyes and the insistent light of the full moon seeped through her wagon canopy. The crying continued.

Iris jammed her bare feet into Oren's rough boots and pulled on his heavy overcoat. She climbed painfully over the canvas drawstring and lowered herself to the ground. She followed the sound, trying in vain to be silent, secretive; the thud crunch of the heavy boots on the uneven ground sounded to Iris like cannon blasts in the still night. When safely out of camp, she ran. Ignoring the pain that still sliced through her womb, ignoring the drops of blood that still trickled down her legs, she ran across sagebrush and stumbled over boulders.

A shadowy figure, with long braids that flew in the moonlight, appeared out of nowhere and ran in front of her, leading the way. Iris ran as dreamers run, with legs that pump without muscles. The crying grew louder, and Iris ran faster to overtake the shadowy figure. "You can't have him again," she said to the dark shape. Desperately, she lunged at the flying braids, snagging one of them with her wedding ring. The figure disappeared. The crying stopped.

Iris whirled around, pressing down the panic in her mouth with both fists. She sank to her knees. The moon had followed her. She looked up to see the leaves on the topmost branches of the quaking aspen trembling. But the earthward branches were passive. Still. Like Iris.

A wolf had followed her too. She smelled his damp coat in the darkness and heard the pad of his footsteps in the dead leaves. The circles he made around her were growing ever smaller. Soon he would be on her, and then it would be over.

Iris could not move. She covered her face with her arms when he snarled and lunged.

"Kill-dee!" a bird shrieked just a foot from her head. It was brown and white; two black necklaces encircled its throat. "Kill-dee!" it shrieked again as it hobbled away. It held one wing aloft, as if broken, and scrambled across the leaves in front of the wolf. "Kill-dee! Kill-dee!" it cried, flapping its broken wing at the wolf and managing, miraculously, to stay two steps ahead of his ready fangs.

Iris thanked the bird for saving her life and was just about to run back to camp when she heard the crying again. The leaves were crying. The leaves at her fingertips. First softly, and then in ragged streaks of sound, angry and desperate. She tore at them and trembled to find a patch of red wool. She dug faster, unearthing next the green and then the gold, clawing at the muddy blanket with cold and clumsy hands. She blew on her frozen fingers as they brushed and tugged at the wool, already seeing before she saw what she would find there.

A tuft of black hair fluttered under her breath, and then the eyes opened, round and black and terrified.

The wolf was coming back. She could almost feel his breath on her face. Iris knew then what the little bird had tried so valiantly to protect, and vowed to perform at least as well as the bird had to save the baby's life. The wolf's paws crackled behind her. In one movement, Iris snatched up the baby and leapt to her feet. She held him under Oren's overcoat with her left arm and whirled to face the bared teeth and hackled coat. Iris slowly bent to wrap her fingers around a heavy branch. When the wolf advanced, she swung it at his muzzle and caught him square in the mouth. He growled and snapped, furious, wounded, disgraced. It took a moment before he tasted his own blood. He looked surprised, then he lunged again. Iris laughed. She could have ripped his jaws apart with her bare hands. She savored the warmth of the squirming bundle beneath her coat and slowly backed away from the slavering beast, shouting like a man would and clubbing him with her stick whenever he was foolish enough to snap his jaws. Her arms were strong like a man's, amazingly strong, strong enough to save a life with one hand and take one with the other.

The moon followed Iris still, shooting light like lances at the stunned and faltering wolf. It encircled Iris and her infant with a silvery armor and dropped beams like halos on the stony earth, guiding their steps back to safety.

Iris crept past the Mosses' wagon and the Blankenships' and the Linkes' and finally into her own. She unwrapped the overcoat and drew out her angel. He frowned and waved a tight, muddy fist in the air, then latched right on to her breast, sucking with great, noisy gulps and pausing now and then to breathe before he started in again. She gave him both engorged breasts and cried and laughed with love and relief as he nursed. Gradually he slowed, and the intervals between his frantic feedings lengthened. Iris inserted, gently, her index finger between his pursed lips and her breast to release the suction. Then she watched him settle back into her arms with a sigh. She laid him beside her, tucking her quilt all around them. She lay awake all night, afraid that if she took her eyes away from him that he would disappear. She held one hand on his chest to make sure it went up and down; she positioned her cheek next to his softly parted lips to feel the air enter and leave and enter again. He shuddered sometimes in his sleep, and she pulled him closer. He was not Oren's baby, but he would be hers.

"He's an Indian," Eula told Iris the next morning.

"Yes, he is," Iris said.

Dollie scooted off to tell her husband, who rounded up most all the men in the train to pay Iris a call. The wagon master brought a bucketful of water. "It was one of them what kilt your husband," he said. "You jest hand him over here, Mrs. Fane, and we'll nip this little problem in the bud."

Iris laid the baby down behind her and slowly reached beneath Oren's overcoat. Her arms were sore and shaky but she pulled out Oren's shotgun and pointed it at the self-righteous circle of faces peering through the drawstring of her canopy. She tried to speak but couldn't; all her energy was focused on the long cold barrel, holding it steady, finding the trigger.

The crowd gasped and grumbled and broke away. They milled about for a while, with low bleatings about Iris being out of her head, about her putting a curse on the journey, about it being a big mistake that they ever let her come along, but they stopped short when they saw the double barrels of Hattie's shotgun also pointed in their direction. "And if she don't," Hattie said, her own wide-eyed children attached to her like so many dusty petticoats, "I believe I will."

That night Iris shivered with the chills. Hattie brought her blankets and boiled up some bone soup. "I'm scared fer her, and fer that baby," Hattie told her husband. Roy Linke said maybe it would help if they pulled their own wagon right up close to hers, to guard her from intruders and such, so the poor girl could get some sleep. Hattie kissed her husband and told him she was glad she got hitched up with him way back when and not no one else.

Hattie and Roy listened hard half the night, but all was quiet save the hoot of the owls and the howl of an occasional coyote. They neither saw nor heard the shadowy figure that crept into Iris's wagon while she slept.

Iris woke to find it kneeling over her child. The figure's head was bowed, revealing only two thick black ropes of braids that dangled over her sleeping child like lifelines. The figure was clearly a woman; she was dressed in pearl white buckskin with long fringes that shimmied from the yoke and sleeves. She wore bracelets of silver and coral on her slender wrists, and was placing a single *hernava*, a tiny golden rose, over the baby's heart.

"Who are you?" Iris asked. The woman froze, head still bowed, one hand still hovering over the baby. "I won't hurt you," Iris said. She reached out a trembling hand to reassure the woman, but the woman pulled away. They stayed that way for some time. Iris reclined on one elbow, weak and feverish, fingering the butcher knife beneath her pillow; the woman kneeling with her head bowed, her long braids still dangling; the baby wrapped in Isabella's finest linen tablecloth and blanketed with Oren's overcoat, as radiant in his quiet slumber as was the tiny golden rose on his heart. At length Iris spoke again. "What do you want?"

The long white part in the black hair of the Indian woman gradually shortened as she lifted her head. Iris gasped. The woman's face was grotesquely twisted, pulled in unnatural directions by a jagged diagonal scar. Much of her nose was missing and half of her mouth fell off to the side, exposing rotting teeth and blackened gums. Tears puddled in the woman's eyes. She pointed to her mouth and shook her head.

Iris moved to touch her again, but again she edged away. The woman reached under her long skirt and pulled out a pearl white pouch. It was decorated with tiny orbs of coral. Slowly she tugged at the leather thongs, then eased her hand inside and pulled out the gift. This she carried in her clenched fist to Iris. She turned her fist over and appeared to be trying to smile, managing only a grimace that further exposed her teeth and yanked at the corner of her right eye so that the white of it looked like a heavy moon splashing into a crimson sea.

Iris held out her hand to receive the offering. In it was dropped a plain brown stone. The woman closed Iris's fingers around it, then, with a touch like a breeze, settled Iris back on her pillow and silently bade her sleep.

When Hattie checked on Iris the next morning, she was sitting straight up and smiling. The baby's brown head was already attached to Iris's white breast. "Climb up," Iris called. "Hurry."

Hattie clucked and cooed and smoothed Iris's hair as she listened to her tale about the woman in white, but when Iris showed her the stone, still clutched in her hand, now bright and green as new clover in Virginia, Hattie quick shoved it down and told her not to be flashing that god-damned emerald around lest someone should kill her for it.

Most of the above is purely factual but, to be honest, it does get a bit blurry for me as soon as Singing Bird shows up. You'll have to take my mother's word for all those ferocious wolf and necklaced bird and buried baby and magic moonlight parts, just as I always have, since that whole little ballad changed the world for my mother and why would she lie?

You'll be relieved to learn that my father's story is quite a bit easier to swallow. It is straightforward and direct, and relatively short, much like my father himself. Oren Fane, as you have most likely figured out for yourself, was not my father. He was just the unstable, albeit romantic, vehicle of transportation of my mother to my father. Not unlike a covered wagon when you think about it.

My father's name was Angus Dwelly Baldoon. He fled Scotland with his first wife, Ellen, and his twin sons, Elgin and Glen, and a clutch of other Scottish settlers to try their luck in the New Land. They settled in the Northern part of Kansas, called their new home the Scottish Plains, and lived rather contentedly until they realized that trouble, like the plague of grasshoppers that devoured their first harvest, like the snow that froze their second, like the rain that flooded their third, sometimes fell from the very skies and landed right smack on their lives regardless of where they planted themselves.

On the day the Baldoons left for America, Ellen carefully folded and rolled her lace curtains. Mr. Baldoon gathered up his fishing gear and grunted and sighed as he struggled to consolidate it into the smallest possible package. Ellen's mother gazed out the naked window and did not speak; her daughter tucked an afghan about her mother's legs then turned back to the cupboard to determine how much of her silver and linens could be stuffed into the big copper kettle.

Elgin and Glen did not realize, as they packed, that this move meant the end of their midnight forays to Edenkillie cave, that never again would they be using their father's red silk handkerchiefs to torment poor old King, Mr. Corygill's lame and nearsighted bull. Everything was going to change for them but they couldn't have known that then. They were cheering and whistling and poking each other slyly as they folded their best starched shirts and hid them, along with their woolen socks and shiny Sunday shoes, under a loose floor plank. They wouldn't be needing those things anymore. They were going to live with the Indians.

My mother always called my father Mr. Baldoon, at least in front of us. He looked like a Mr. Baldoon. I remember him as being always old and shrunken and scrawny, with legs that bowed like a sailor's and peachy-gray whiskers that grew straight from his mustache into his sideburns and tickled when he held you in his lap. Everyone loved Mr. Baldoon. Especially my mother and me. And, it must be said, Boy Found.

Dark River struck Singing Bird when he found out. He struck her four times so that thin streams of blood made lacy designs on her perfect face and ran into small perfect pools in the snow where she'd fallen. He struck her mother too, and cursed her, and sent her from their tipi for allowing it to happen.

Dark River held Runs Swiftly by the shoulders and stood him in front of Chief One on the Wind. Dark River spoke with his eyes to the chief and to the elders. Black-Faced Bear sat next to the chief and listened intently. Singing Bird was his betrothed. He was the party most grievously wronged. He would have Runs Swiftly's penis and Singing Bird's heart. He would have those parts of them in his hands and he would spit on them and he would throw them to the dogs. He had always hated Runs Swiftly. He had always loved Singing Bird. He glared at his father, Chief One on the Wind, and passed him his thoughts with his eyes.

Chief One on the Wind looked up to the heavens, then nodded to each man in turn, grateful for the wisdom their collective thoughts had given him. He rose and spoke. "Esteemed elders, and Honorable braves," he began. "Hear my judgment. Runs Swiftly has taken that which belongs to another. He has behaved in a womanly fashion, deceiving us in the darkness, shaming his father and my only son. For this betrayal of the Men Among Men, he shall be banished from our midst for three Snow Moons. When the waters flow again, he may, if repentant, return to us."

Black-Faced Bear leapt to his feet. "My father!" he shouted. "That cannot be enough! What of my honor!"

Chief One on the Wind waved his son down. "You interrupt me, my son. You shall not speak again until I have finished." The long creases running down the chief's face deepened as he spoke of Singing Bird. "She was our favored child," he began again. "She gave us song and light and morning, and we shall miss her. But the wrong she has committed is a great one. And her station, as daughter of Dark River, as hope of my heart, as betrothed to a chief's son, dictates that the price she pays for that wrong must also be a great one. For sharing her beauty with Runs Swiftly, she shall have that beauty no more. For saving her songs for his ears alone, she shall sacrifice them forever. For loving one man above her own people and pride, she shall be shunned by those people and stripped of that pride." Chief One on the Wind stirred the last burning embers of the fire and picked up a white-hot stone. He held it in his bare fingers and showed it to every member of the council. "For her presumption in wanting more than I have already given her, she shall carry this Stone of Life with her always, or until she finds another willing to bear its burden."

Black-Faced Bear smiled. Chief One on the Wind drew the knife from Dark River's belt and laid it in the fire. "You shall have the honor," he told Singing Bird's father.

Black-Faced Bear leapt up again. "I must claim that honor, Father." Dark River's mouth trembled imperceptibly, and he bowed to Black-Faced Bear's demand.

Chief One on the Wind nodded, then turned to Runs Swiftly. "Bring the girl," he said.

Even Hattie was surprised by my mother's obstinacy when it came to naming the baby.

"Boy Found," Iris insisted. "I'm calling him Boy Found because that's what he is." They sat by the river, and Iris rinsed and soaped and pounded the Indian blanket with rocks as she spoke. "Indians like descriptive names," she said. "Oren told me."

"But how about your pa's name," Hattie said, "or your uncle's? Something more like regular folks?"

Iris ignored her friend and spread the blanket on a large boulder to dry. "And when he distinguishes himself, as I know he will," she said, smiling down at the baby, "he will take a new name."

If only I could have been there that day, I would have argued on Hattie's side. Names mean a lot, I think. They pull you around and steer you crash bang into your destiny. Henry would have been lovely. Or John, or Charley, or William. Even Oliver. But Boy Found. Might as well have hung a sign around his neck that said I Am No One. Might as well have given him a rope with one end tied to hell and told him to hang on for dear life. If only my mother could have foreseen how fast and hard Boy Found was going to have to ride in order to escape that name. If only she could have known about the way he was to distinguish himself, about the new name he was later, after everything happened, to be saddled with. If only she could have known, back then, about me.

But she couldn't have known. She could only go on, so that's what she did. She had considered, when Oren died, returning to Virginia, to her mother and father, to her pale sisters, to the pretty young men in the cool shade of the Spanish moss dripping from the oaks overhead, and regaling them all with her wild tales of the frontier. She imagined how they would drop their jaws in amazement and pat her hand in sympathy and speak of her courage and strength and fetch her cool drinks and darken her room when she napped and give a grand ball in celebration of her triumphant return. But after that night in the woods and the discovery of Boy Found, her visions of the homecoming altered in significant ways, not the least of which was the inclusion of a brown baby in her arms in all of those pictures, and she realized that it was the cool shade of those trees that tugged at her most. Certainly that was not worth trading her baby for.

So she continued. She kept her shotgun near her in the wagon while nursing and carried the butcher knife always in the pocket of her apron. She trusted no one except Hattie and Roy.

Hattie told Roy about the emerald. Roy found a length of coarse chain to make a long necklace. That way Iris could keep her treasure close and away from prying eyes. He told Hattie to bring him the jewel so he could drill a hole for the chain, but she brought him only a smooth gray rock, cool as metal. "Some emerald," he said when Hattie dropped it in his hand. They shook their heads.

"My eyes must have been playing tricks on me," Hattie said.

Roy drilled the stone with great care nevertheless (although he broke two drill bits in the process and cursed the stone same way he did his mules) and then finally he slipped the chain through and soldered the ends together in the fire. "There," he said, handing the finished necklace to Hattie. "Now at least she won't lose it."

A blizzard hit just as they were creeping through Purgatory Pass. The wagon train was forced to sit tight and just wait and worry, and everyone's faith started to unravel. Most families were already down to their last couple pounds of grease and flour, and by day seven were losing their good judgment. That day brought an unexpected and eerie kind of celebration when one of the Blankenships' horses keeled over. There was a public feast, of sorts, on the carcass. Not that the Blankenships invited anyone to join them, but they were as gracious as could be expected when they saw that they had no choice. Fact is, the whole thing fell short of expectations; by the time the carcass was stripped and boned and divvied up, there wasn't really all that much to go around. And besides, most of it didn't set well in their empty stomachs and came right back up again anyways.

The eldest Blankenship boy grained and stretched and treated the hide, then paraded all around camp with it flung over his shoulders. He boasted to everyone he saw that he had made it for "his woman." This relieved the monotony somewhat, at least for the pretty young girls who giggled about it when together and who, individually, for romantic and more practical reasons, clasped their icy fingers together each night and begged their God to be the one Holl Blankenship sought.

They called him Holl, this handsome and pretentious boy. It might have been short for something more pompous—Hollonious, perhaps, or Hollowaverly—but Holl was all my mother ever heard anyone call him, and Holl was enough for her to remember for the rest of her life. He was sixteen years old, well-formed and big for his age, and crowned with wavy black hair that he often allowed to linger alluringly over one eye before tossing it back again. Although his father had now and then felt obliged to beat some sense into the boy for sassing the wagon master or for cussing at his mother, Holl was the secret hope and delight of both his parents, and they would have gladly offered up their own carcasses to his appetites if it ever came to that.

Iris had not been much aware of his presence until that awful blizzard, but by the twelfth day in Purgatory Pass, frostbite had claimed six toes, influenza had claimed four young children, and Holl Blankenship had claimed Iris as "his woman." She thought he was mocking her the first time he approached. He crept up behind and touched her hair. When she whirled around, he caught her shoulders and gazed at her with such melodramatic anguish that she laughed and patted his head, then climbed back into her wagon to attend to Boy Found. She couldn't know that he would interpret her reaction as a challenge that he could not, with honor, ignore.

He started leaving little presents in her wagon. A cracker one day, which Iris gave to Greta, Hattie's youngest. A branch of holly the next. The day after, a lock of black hair. Iris shuddered as she shook the hair off Oren's overcoat onto the snow; she decided it was time to have a talk with the boy. The stinging snow had eased a bit, so after supper she bundled up Boy Found and trudged through the drifts to the Blankenships' wagon. She found Holl astride a very black, very thin horse. Holl's own mane was waving in the darkening wind. He was grinning down at three shivering girls wrapped in their fathers' heaviest coats, assuring them that all would yet be well, that he would get them all out of this fearsome predicament, that he would personally buy each one of them a powder blue satin gown with a pink satin sash and three petticoats the minute they got to a halfway respectable town.

Iris cleared her throat. "Excuse me, Holl," she said. "Can I see you a minute?"

Holl lifted one long leg over the stallion's head and slipped to the ground before the "Yes ma'am" made it out of his mouth. He shouldered his way through his trio of admirers as if they were trees and kept going until he was right up close to my mother.

Iris took two steps backward and smiled at the three girls, who were no longer giggling. "Holl . . ." she urged, indicating the indignant Holl-worshipers he no longer seemed to see. Slowly, with irritation, he shifted his gaze to the three figures with their hands planted on their hips. "Git," he said, jerking his head at them. They moved away, back to their wagons, sulking, swinging their hips deliberately and with great difficulty in the deep snow, determined to make their anger and their unappreciated appeal visible beneath their bulky man-coats. From time to time they twisted their heads around to shoot furious glances over their shoulders. Not at Holl, but at Iris.

"You could have been more polite," Iris said.

Holl's gaze had settled back on her mouth. "No, I couldn't," he said.

"Listen to me," Iris began. She took a deep breath and tried to remember how to make her voice sound kind. "You're a very nice boy, Holl. But you're going to be hurt if you don't . . ."

"I ain't a boy," he said, placing a finger on her lips. "And you're the one who is gonna be hurt if you don't." His mouth slid into a smile then, and he paused to let his curling forelock linger in front of his eyes.

As he sidled in closer, Iris tightened her grip on Boy Found and groped with her right hand for the butcher knife in the pocket of Oren's overcoat. "You're making a mistake," she said, and when she felt his eager breath on her face and his fingers fumbling with her buttons she remembered the wolf in the forest, and the blood she had drawn then, and slowly, she slid the knife out of her pocket and lifted it up, slow, to his throat and then jab pricked him right under the chin, and when he gasped, she held it there, and thought about her dead husband and her dead son and about the high probability of her own death, stuck there in the dead white snow, trapped in an impassable pass, and then she held the knife there a moment longer and pressed a little harder, for she was a good woman, through and through, which is a whole lot more than I turned out to be.

"Jesus," said Holl. "You really are crazy." And then my mother abandoned him again. She left him standing there alone with nothing but white beneath him and black overhead and fine, flying splinters of ice pricking his face and neck like thousands of tiny knives. They hurt him more, in truth, than the one she had used, but they couldn't fly straight to his pride as hers had, and she would pay for the wound she'd inflicted.

Hattie made Iris and Boy Found bunk in with their family for the night. "No telling what that boy will be up to next," Roy said. The wind howled and screamed outside, but the jumble of bodies molded itself into a soft, warm heap. Hattie pulled half a loaf of stale bread out from under some pots and pans. "I been savin' this," she said, then broke it into little crumbly bits to pass around.

Iris chewed a long time on her tiny portion. "Just like you keep on saving me," she said. She started to speak again, but just shook her head. She nursed Hattie's little Greta that night, along with Boy Found.

Hattie patted four-year-old Greta as she suckled. "We're all family here," she reassured her.

Iris slept better that night than she had in months, tossed with her baby into that sea of flailing limbs, of slumbering community breaths, of tangled blankets. She dreamt of soft summers spent in Virginia, where the gentle waters sometimes lapped at your feet, but never swept you away. As she slept, the Life Stone grew warm on her breast, and when she woke up next morning it was yellow as the sun.

"Git up!" a voice shouted. "Rise and shine! There's gonna be a weddin'!" Iris climbed over the barely stirring bodies and poked her head out the back of the wagon. Holl was jumping around in the snow, banging on a frying pan with a stirring spoon, jabbering something about his woman.

His ma and pa were right behind him, scowling and poking their noses into everyone's wagons and shouting, "Where is she? Where is the witch?"

Hattie yanked Iris back inside, then stuck her own head out. "What are y'all fussin' about? Pipe down, can't ya?"

Eula Blankenship raced over to Hattie and started wagging her finger in her face. "It's your fault, Hattie Linke! It's your fault that boy over there is full out of his head!" Eula was sobbing now and wringing her hands. "She's a witch, I tell you! And you been helpin' her! Mark my words! One of these days your children goin' to wake up with horns sprung right out of their heads. And don't think she'll spare them, neither!" She slumped against Hattie's wagon and watched helplessly as Holl continued to shout and jump in the snow. "No ma'am," she said more to herself than to Hattie, "She ain't gonna spare a one a them."

Ed Blankenship was still poking his head in everyone's wagon and slinging swear words like pebbles at pigeons. "There it is!" he shouted. "There's proof for all you soft-headed fools!" He reached into Iris's wagon and pulled out Holl's horsehide, holding it high over his head and waving it from side to side like a flag.

"Iris!" Holl called then. "I made that just for you. Ain't for no one else. It's a present for . . . for last night."

The younger Blankenship boys hooted appreciatively and slapped each other on the back in tribute to their brother's prowess. Eula clutched her heart, and Ed hurled the horsehide to the ground shouting, "There, harlot! Show your face and win your prize!"

Roy Linke had quietly drawn the wagon master aside and appeared to be explaining something. The wagon master nodded, then turned and folded his arms across his chest to watch the show. Roy tied my mother's favorite bay to his team. He took her shotgun and a couple of boxes out of her wagon and loaded them into his own. He counted heads to make sure that Hattie and Iris and all the children were safe inside, then he checked the mules' and horses' harnesses and hooves, and rubbed their legs vigorously with his gloved hands.

Ed was still fuming, Eula still sobbing, Holl and his brothers were still jumping around and congratulating themselves when the sun, big and hot and yellow, muscled its way out from behind the clouds. It pushed the sky apart and filled up the spaces with a warmth, like peace, that settled softer than snowflakes on the dark and narrow pass.

"Hallelujah," Hattie whispered. It seemed like the trees started to thaw right then and there—the heavy icicles blinked into soft, fat drops; the wind sighed into silence; and even the snow, packed and entwined around the wagon wheels like choking vines, at last retreated and sank quietly, obligingly, back into the earth.

"Holl, look!" cried one of his giggly girls. "It's a miracle!" cried another. "It happened just like you said it would!" cried the third.

They were pointing at the sun, but Holl was not looking at the sun. He was suddenly still, noticing Roy Linke for the first time. "No, you don't," he said. "She's not gettin' off that easy."

Roy held fast to the lead and helped his team pick its way out of the snow. "Where you goin'?" Holl demanded.

Roy climbed up on top of the wagon and snapped the reins. "Giddap," he said to the team. "Away," he said to Holl.

"To hell, I hope!" Holl watched their slow escape, increasingly aware of the abrupt silence in the camp and of the many eyes now focused in his direction. He ran for the wagon with heavy, effortful strides in the deep snow. With a forced, self-conscious agility, he managed to hook one hand in the canopy and hoist himself up onto the back. Hattie pried him off once with a rusty shovel, but he repeated the performance a second time. "I wanna talk to Iris," he said.

Iris motioned to Hattie to let him speak.

"Well, talk fast then," Hattie said.

Holl pulled himself halfway inside, his words bouncing and cracking with the jostling wagon. "I jest wanted you to know," he began, "sweet darlin'," and here his grin changed into something twisted and ugly, like something that had been cut in half, "that this is what you git for laughin' at me." He reached in farther, as if to touch her face, but grabbed a hank of her hair instead and pulled hard until Hattie's shovel made him let go. Then he fell back into the snow laughing, laughing at the sudden coldness on his back, laughing at the wagon as it rolled on without him, laughing at Iris for thinking she could walk away from Holl Blankenship without so much as a backward glance—and he had to wait in the snow like that a good four minutes before his parents got there, red-faced and huffing, to pick him up again.

It wasn't until they were some way off that Iris had a chance to mourn those pieces of her past that Roy had not been able to smuggle away. Her candlesticks had not been saved, nor had her mother's down pillows. It made her sick to realize that Oren's hat had been left behind and that Holl was probably pawing through her things and staining that cream-colored felt with the oil of his filthy hair at that very moment. But she still had Boy Found and she still had the Life Stone, and she pressed both to her heart and thanked God for that.

Hattie called up to Roy, "Where we goin'?" Roy just shrugged and kept on talking to the mules. It was all Iris's fault, the whole mess, and Iris knew it. When Greta started whining that they were all of them lost and going to die, Hattie slapped her hand, but Iris pulled the little girl over and nursed her again.

When Greta and Boy Found had each taken what they needed from her breasts, Iris called to Roy to let her drive the team a piece. She bundled up and crawled out of the wagon while Roy blew inside his gloves. He made sure she held the reins right before he climbed in and wedged himself between the bodies in the tight, warm niche she had left for him.

"Hah," she said to the mules. The bay looked over her shoulder at her and snorted. Iris knew what she meant; she felt the same way. They were all of them lost and going to die, just like Greta said. But in the meantime, she could still keep the wagon rolling and she could still feel the sun on her shoulders. "Hah!" she said to the bay, louder this time, cracking the whip in the still air.

As morning rolled into afternoon, the Life Stone grew warmer on her breast. The sun stretched and swelled until it blocked out all the blue. Iris tugged her bonnet farther down over her eyes, but the reflected glare from the bright snow was by midday nearly blinding.

There was no trail that Iris could see, so she steered the wagon between the trees and bushes and trusted, without much faith, to the instincts of the mules. She and Roy and Hattie took shifts driving the team, and by the second day were more dismayed than elated to realize that not one of the other wagons had followed them.

At least the snow was still melting. It gave them fresh water and gradually uncovered edible roots and plants. These bitter snacks, along with the white rabbit Hattie shot and skinned, lifted their spirits considerably.

Still, they were definitely lost. "No gettin' around it," Roy told Hattie. Iris spent a fitful night during which she dreamt of Holl—not of Holl exactly, but of a block of mud covered with black wavy grass and with Holl's hands, torn from its bank, bounding and crashing over rapids, dropping pieces of itself as it whirled. She woke early and rose before the others to start the fire for breakfast.

She heard a rustle in the darkness; she threw a rock in its direction, then turned back to her task. She sat on a boulder and set about coaxing first tiny sparks, and then feeble flames, from the damp kindling. When dawn broke, she warmed her hands at the fragile fire and drew out the Life Stone to examine it in private. It had taken on a coral hue, the color of the newly awakening sky. When she touched it to her lips Iris was surprised to feel a cool, misty moisture.

A flash of white skirted past; Iris leapt to her feet and whirled around. She moved instinctively, cautiously in the semidarkness. Once more she was rewarded with that flash of white. She quickened her pace, but saw only vast and murky space ahead. That and the sharp line of the horizon marking the lethal division between earth and sky.

It was a steep cliff, Iris saw. A steep cliff with a single sycamore growing perilously close to the edge. And the sycamore had two branches that looked like arms. The arms moved, almost. Almost beckoned. They pointed to the left. The bark on its trunk was pearly white and peeling off in places like fringe. Then Iris rubbed her eyes and the sun flew up, erasing all the shadows. Boy Found cried for his breakfast.

Roy and Hattie climbed down from the wagon and sat by the fire. As they sighed into their wild-root tea, Iris told them, "I know how to get out of here."

My brothers and I laughed later on when our mother told us these stories. Just picturing her—all tiny and birdlike and, to us, gullible as all get-out—actually beating off wolves, or holding a knife to anyone's throat, or lifting a huge gray shotgun like the one our father kept on the wall and pointing it at regular grown-up white people was enough to make us laugh with our mouths wide open until we nearly burst our water. But our mother would laugh then too. First at herself and then at us, braying like mules and rolling in the grass. And Mr. Baldoon, if he happened along, would kiss my mother on the top of her head then tickle our ribs with the tip of his boot, just in case we were losing our gumption to laugh ourselves sick.

Boy Found had already left by then. I was too young at the time to remember the parting, but my elder brother, Hugh, remembered. He told me about it once when we were up in the hayloft, hiding from Henry. He told me how Boy Found had slipped away one night without telling anyone, and how our mother used to wander far out into the grasses and just stand there in the wind, looking around, looking at nothing as far as he and Henry could tell, until our father would go out after her, calling to Hugh to mind Henry, leaning into the wind, carrying me in his arms with his hat over my face, to bring her back again.

"He weren't much to me, though," Hugh said then. And the way he shrugged his shoulders and chewed on that straw when he said it made me think that maybe I should be glad that Boy Found had left.

It was the crossing of rivers that Iris hated most. The first few hadn't been too bad. Oren had been with her then, and the water was shallow enough where the wagon master led them. But then Oren died and the rivers got deeper. Each one was deeper than the last, and each time she held onto the wagon with whiter knuckles and tighter resolve to keep from throwing herself into the water all in one piece and be done with it. More and more, that seemed preferable to risking yet another chunk of her spirit being torn away and swallowed up in the muddy waters. The last crossing was the worst, and for that reason Iris determined that it would be the last, come what may.

It was the Big Blue that decided her. The Linkes were bound for Oregon and Iris had planned on staying with them, but the Big Blue changed all that. The river was still swollen from the snowmelt, and although they camped on the east bank for three days waiting for it to subside, the water just kept roaring and rushing on. Large dead logs washed by, and dead birds, and one dead buffalo.

"I can't," Iris told Roy. He patted her hand then set about driving the animals farther downstream where, he said, the Big Blue would be gentling down.

"Here we are," Roy said when they rounded a bend four days later. "This corner should slow her a bit."

It didn't look any slower to Iris, but Hattie seemed satisfied. Hattie commenced tying ropes around the children's waists and then attaching them to Iris. "You mind the younguns in the wagon," Hattie told her. "I'll help Roy get the team across."

Iris started to object, then stopped herself. Hattie was right. Iris would be useless up front, pulling mules through icy water. She'd need to be strong to do that, to be brave, to keep her eyes open the whole time no matter what. Iris was neither strong nor brave, and tears burned in her eyes as she lashed Boy Found across her breast and called the children into the wagon.

Roy cussed at the mules as he dragged them into the water. Hattie hit them with switches and scolded them as if they were naughty children. The bay mare was tied to the back of the wagon, where her own stubbornness wouldn't influence the mules. Iris watched her snort and rear and roll her incredulous eyes as the dust she kicked up in protest gradually turned into splashes of water, then into water too deep to splash.

The Big Blue pounded against the right side of the wagon and Greta's eyes popped open round and gray as she squealed in delight. Iris dug her fingernails into the wood of the wagon and smiled at Greta. It wasn't so bad. It wouldn't be so bad. Roy kept cussing and Hattie kept scolding. The terror in the bay's eyes had been replaced by the customary contempt. Iris relaxed a moment and rechecked the knots in the ropes.

Then the cussing stopped abruptly and Hattie screamed. Iris watched the bay veer out of the small circle of her vision. Greta cried out for her mama and then Iris was lying on her side with two children on top of her, her hair wet, and her left arm pinned beneath her. Water seeped through the canvas into her ear, her nose. She pushed the children off and told them to hold on. Then the river screamed, "Mamamama," before it reached up and pulled her under and struck her face, her stomach, with great silent fists of water and wrapped her skirts like lassos around her legs, and Boy Found was all she could think of, Boy Found, strapped to her breast and still, silent, not even struggling, and she had to get him up, away, out and she clawed at the icy fingers tearing at her lungs and she kicked at the black hands pulling on her feet and she swam toward the light, toward the air, and the cottonwoods were still there, above her, waving blurry in the wind, and then, one more kick, and she broke through at last the watery membrane that divided the bleary from the clear and she choked on the sharp air and she thrust her breast to the sky patting and entreating Boy Found to breathe, breathe until he choked and coughed too, and then she saw Hattie's four children, still tied to her, bobbing about like corks.

"Mama," Greta cried again, and Iris tugged on the ropes as she treaded water, to pull them near. They were all crying except for seven-year-old Josiah. He was watching the wagon spinning down the river like a toy boat, dragging the lifeless bay in its wake.

Iris could no longer feel her legs, but she kept them kicking anyway as she scratched and tore at her heavy skirt until it finally let go of her bodice. She watched as the billow of forest green linen dove and danced after the wagon. Then she lay on her back, Boy Found cradled on her chest, Hattie's children in tow, and kicked for shore.

The cottonwoods along the shore seemed to be near but kept retreating. At one point she nearly grabbed hold of an overhanging branch, but then the current swept them out again. Her legs felt as numb as they had that night in the forest, and her lungs were freezing up. Hattie's children were sinking.

"Please," she said to the Big Blue, and made one more desperate lunge for a branch of cottonwood. This time she caught it, or it caught her, and she pulled, or it pulled, because then she was crawling in the mud and then winding in Hattie's children like wash on a line.

Greta said she saw an angel. Later on, when they were dry and warm and grieving, Greta said she saw an angel pulling on my mother's hand. But Roy didn't hear and the other children didn't care and Iris just kept rubbing the Life Stone, now cold and black as death, between her palms. She rubbed it feverishly, incessantly, as if warming it up and changing its color might somehow bring Hattie back again.

I could have saved her a lot of energy. I could have told her that you can't bring back anything once it's gone, Life Stone or not. Where my mother went wrong, and little Greta too, was in mistaking Singing Bird for something benevolent, an angel. In truth she was just the opposite. A voiceless siren. A demon dressed in white.

The Life Stone is not a good-luck piece. It is not a talisman against evil, not a protective amulet, not a window into the future, not even a mirror of the present. What it is, exactly, is more difficult to explain. It is a something like a magnet in that it has the power to attract. But unlike a magnet, the Life Stone is never content with attracting iron alone—it pulls in everything, everywhere, every ecstasy, every torment, and offers up each to its wearer bathed in lights, in truths, in colors too vivid, too exquisite to be either ignored or endured. The Life Stone grants its wearer the gift of Life. That's all. Not a good life, not a happy life, not even a long life. But a full life, filled to bursting, like an overblown carnival balloon, like a cow's belly stuffed with grain, like a compost heap left too long in the sun. And whoever might be shattered or splattered by the explosion, whoever might be singed by the flames or even burnt up completely, is of no concern to the Life Stone. No more than it is to Singing Bird.

Downriver, Roy was beached on the back of a mule. By the time Iris and the children found him, both he and the mule were spouting water and waking up. He went to the edge of the Big Blue and peered into its swirling center. He found a long dead branch and jabbed into its heart. He looked like an ancient wizard stirring a giant churning cauldron. He looked like a tired, broken man fishing for something that would not be there.

"Go away," he said to Iris, but his voice was soft as moss.

They wandered farther downriver. Josiah found my mother's green skirt snagged on a branch. Then they saw the overturned wagon wedged between two boulders. The bloated carcass of the bay mare rammed up against it, and the Big Blue shot clear over the horse's neck like a waterfall.

Roy climbed over the boulders and handed supplies from the wagon to Iris. He passed her blankets, a cooking pot, his other pair of pants (he told her to put them on), and the last few pieces of jerky. Then he climbed out again, carrying the small tin box that held their savings. "Hattie will skin me if I don't take this," he said. He walked briskly along the bank, ahead of the rest of them. His lips kept moving but they made no sound.

He didn't speak again until he found her. And then all he said was "No." Hattie's body also was wedged between boulders, and the river leapt over her face as it had the bay's neck. Her right arm was caught in the current and pointed downstream; her plump hand fluttered gracefully in the rippling water like a rainbow trout. Roy pulled her out. Iris covered her with one of the blankets before her children saw her bloated face; her sunken, glassy eyes; her foam white lips.

At the end of the Big Blue was the Kansas River, and that forked back up into the Republican. Iris was surrounded. "I'm staying here with Hattie," she told Roy.

They were bunking with a small family in a large cabin a couple of miles from Hattie's grave. They had managed, with the help of W. B. Gruver and his son, Lem, to get the wagon back on the bank. Two wheels were badly crushed and one whole side was nothing but splinters, but Roy and W. B. and Lem sawed and sanded and shaped and nailed until they had a passable sturdy wagon once again.

Iris spent her days stitching up the canvas. She wanted to do more. She wanted to salvage something of Hattie to comfort her motherless children, something they could touch and smell and carry with them into their beds at night. But all Iris found was a brass bell pull (carried all that long way to ornament the door of their new home in Oregon, Iris supposed), and an old peg lamp. Everything else had been abandoned to make room for food and tools on the long trip. "A sad legacy," Iris said to W. B., but she said it real quiet because Hattie would have thrown a fit if she'd heard. Hattie took along everything she'd needed. And she'd managed to keep them all alive besides.

Mildred Gruver kept to herself most of the time. She shut herself up in a back room, unraveling old sweaters brought from the east then mixing the wools and knitting them back into tight new garments, often without neck or sleeve openings, often lacking discernible shapes, which she folded as neatly as possible without shoulder seams to guide her and stacked in the basement near the potato bin.

Lem did all the fishing, hunting, cooking, and housework. "Oh, Lem!" Mildred Gruver called sometimes. Used to be that Lem would run to her, thinking that she needed him. But then she'd just stare at him when he got there, as if she didn't know who he was, and then she'd start picking the lint off his clothes and rolling it into little balls, so that after a while he didn't go see her anymore except to bring her meals.

W. B. tended the vegetable garden on Saturdays, read poetry to Mildred on Sundays, and filled the other five days of each week with adding rooms to their cabin. It took the form of an addiction, this perpetual supplementation, this desperate transformation of forest to home, of tree to log to house, as if the additions could fill in a lack. As if more shelter could protect his Mildred from the invisible demons that crawled in through the windows and chimneys and plucked out her hair.

W. B. took it upon himself to aid and abet any lost or weary traveler, be he outlaw or Christian, savage or man, that stumbled onto his land. He dropped his hammer and ran, therefore, when he sighted the hard-put party of settlers that appeared, as if out of a dream, from behind the wild purple phlox.

Mildred saw them too. She watched their slow approach from her tiny back window. But she didn't leave her room or even wave a greeting, just pulled back out of sight, leaned against the cold wall, and laughed. She stretched out her long spidery arms and then brought them together with a loud smack. "Saved," she said.

Iris saw the lanky figure slip from view as they approached, but was more interested in the oaks and maples and cottonwoods and elms that surrounded the ranging cabin. She was carrying Greta by then too, along with Boy Found, and the luscious shade of those sheltering branches, and the fragrant smoke rising from the chimney below called to her with the low, throbbing song of the whippoorwill.

When Roy announced at dinner one night that it was time to move on to Oregon, Iris told him of her decision to stay. She was not surprised when he just nodded and kept chewing on a tough piece of stewed venison.

She was surprised, however, when Mildred came flying up from the basement, waving her skinny arms and shrieking like her hair was on fire. She hit the floor hard with her knees and wound her arms around Roy's boots. "Take me!" she cried, and her voice grated like a fork on a tin plate.

W. B. rushed to unwind her. Lem looked down at his supper. "Don't be scared," W. B. told Iris. "She ain't right, that's all." He petted her sparse and graying hair. "Ain't been right since Lem's brother got drowned." Mildred broke from his arms and ran outside. She ran straight to the wagon and climbed inside. W. B. ran after her.

"No use," he told Roy and Lem when he came back. "She's set on goin'." He gave Roy a cigar from a box on the hearth.

Iris boiled up some coffee in the kitchen as the men smoked. Then she brought it in and stood before W. B. "I could buy it from you," she said.

W. B. gazed into his coffee.

"I could buy this place from you," Iris said. "For me and Boy Found. And then you could take your wife away."

W. B. looked up at her and frowned.

"I have gold," Iris said.

W. B. set his mug on the hearth and slowly rose to his feet. "What would I want with gold?" he said, still frowning. He padded around the room, pausing now and then to touch the black walnut bookcase, the brick hearth, the real glass windows he and Lem had put in themselves. He ran his fingers down the ivory keys of the piano. "All I want is in that wagon," he said.

Lem stood up and squashed his cigar butt in the fireplace.

W. B. hurried out of the cabin and into the meadow. Lem hung his head and then straightened up again. "Gold will buy us a fine doctor for Ma," he said to Iris. "We will be honored to accept fair payment for this here property."

As it turned out, Lem was able to coax his father out of the meadow and into the journey west. With her four gold coins (W. B. pressed two of them back into her hand but Iris slipped them into Lem's pocket when W. B. looked away), Iris bought the log cabin and the sixty acres that surrounded it. In exchange for the transport of himself and his family to a real city where people lived and went to church and to barn-raisings and where Mildred might get better, W. B. donated three fresh horses (including his new appaloosa), a cartonful of dried milk, six baskets of dried raspberries, and all the put-up tomatoes and acorn squash they could carry.

Iris had to rub her finger all over with lard to get her wedding ring off. "This is for Greta," she told Roy. She wrapped it up in parchment and put it in Roy's metal box. Greta latched on to my mother's skirt with her fists and her teeth while Roy hitched up the horses. My mother cried and kissed

Greta and explained again and again that she was heading off for Oregon where her mama's sister lived, and where her mama had wanted her children to be raised up. But Greta finally had to be pried away by force.

Iris stood with Boy Found in the doorway of her new home and watched the wagon until it rounded the bend at the Republican. Roy and W. B. rode up front, Lem took Josiah with him on the appaloosa, and Mildred huddled in back with the three younger children.

Till her dying day, my mother told me later, she would remember Greta's small face poking out the back of that wagon, dry-eyed by then, and solemn. It was Hattie's face, round and resolute. Those were Hattie's gray eyes. And Iris wished then, wished most desperately after the wagon had already gone too far to chase, wished with a sharpness that pricked her like a wishbone lodged forever in her throat, that she had not let Greta go. Mixed up with that memory, caught forever on that sharp wishbone, was the sound of Mildred's gay, thin, screechy voice singing "She Wore a Yellow Ribbon" as the wagon wheels bumped on the rocky path, and when Mildred got to the part about her lover being far away, her voice pierced the still air of that spring day for Iris far away like the barbed arrow far, far away that had pierced Oren's skull.

The Life Stone rubbed like a burr against my mother's breast, and when she pulled it out, it was pale as the dust that finally, mercifully, smothered Mildred's song.

Jesse came back. Jesse of the wandering longhorns, of the grimy blue neckerchief, of the god-hard biceps that poked out from under those rolled-up sleeves. Jesse, who brushed the corn silk from his thighs. Jesse, whose fingers touched my own when I offered him water from our well.

He came back late one evening, not six weeks after my mother gave me the Life Stone. He pitched pebbles at my window.

Mr. Baldoon was a lighter sleeper than I. He blasted through the door in his nightclothes, firing his shotgun, firing off threats about which part of Jesse he meant to shoot away first, running poor Jesse right off our place.

Jesse came back again, though. Even after all that. The next time was in full daylight, and his neckerchief was all washed and bright, and his hair was slicked back, and he took his hat off when he saw my father. We were just getting home from church, and Jesse was there, leaning against the well, smiling. As I climbed down out of the buggy I noticed that his beautiful teeth looked white as sugar against his coffee brown face.

Mr. Baldoon helped my mother out of the buggy, then made straight for the house and slammed the door behind him. For a minute we all thought he might be after his shotgun again, but when there were no explosions, Jesse kicked his tall pointy boots through the dust to our front door, letting his hand brush against mine on purpose as he passed. And then he knocked.

My mother and I stood still by the buggy, holding our breath. Mr. Baldoon took forever to answer the knock, and when he finally did open that door he looked even older than usual and that's going some. Jesse asked if he could court me, that much I heard, and Mr. Baldoon blustered and sputtered and asked him all sorts of questions without even inviting him in. His lined face was redder than I'd ever seen it, redder even than it was the time Hugh and I set fire to the chicken feed. The way his hands shook frightened me.

"What's wrong with him?" I whispered to my mother. But she was looking out at the corn fields and wouldn't answer me. She knew, though, and it made me furious that she wouldn't answer me straight out. And it makes me mad again just to think of it now, with her seeing all she was seeing: her father grieving on her wedding day, the water rising, the barbed arrow, my own future—and not telling me. Since I had to go ahead and die before I could see it too.

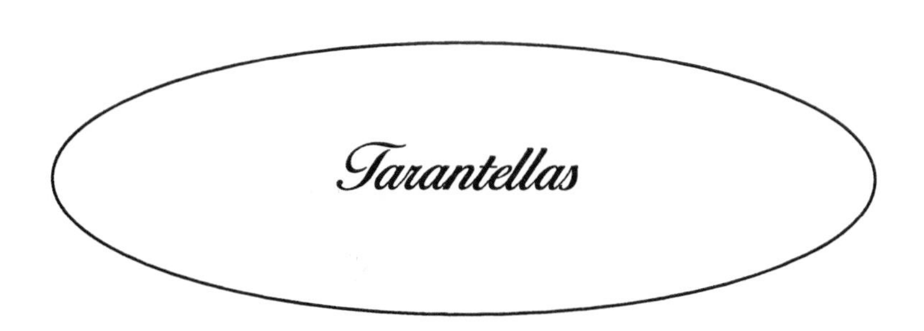

Tarantellas

Runs Swiftly led Singing Bird to the council, and he led her out again when it was over. But he would not look at her when they passed the second time through the flap of the tipi, and he would not speak to her. He tried to keep his thoughts still so they would not go to her, but they were too loud. They battered against his skull like a pronghorn buck, and she heard them. You have shamed me, his downcast eyes told her. And you are hideous. I do not love you now.

She tried to answer his thoughts. But she could not. Not even if her lips were still connected as before. Not even if her tongue were still whole and not the cauterized stump that now wagged side to side behind her teeth. Not even then could she have answered him. She had no thoughts. She felt nothing. They must have cut her heart out too, cut it out and thrown it to the dogs, just as Black-Faced Bear had hoped.

She ran to her tipi, but her mother was not there. Mother! She cried without a voice, but the crying made the blood flow again—the crying made short work of the medicine man's poultices and magic. The blood flowed again, like a stream, like a river, and when Dark River crept back to his wifeless tipi and found his daughter's lifeblood covering his elk-hide robe, he wrapped the hide around himself and rubbed the blood into his own flesh, his own face, reasoning that because he must shun his daughter's body, he would comfort her spirit. For the shame was his as well, and the stain, he vowed, would never be washed from his robe, and he would wear it as she must, until his spirit rose and flew into the sky.

Then he walked far into the forest and sent his thoughts to his wife, to Woman Who Burrows, and he begged her to return, to forgive him, and he scraped sharp rocks against his own seamless face for atonement and he howled at the black sky, howled and moaned and clawed at his belly to be released, released, and he did that all night alone on a rock like a coyote. And the night finally paled into day, but still his spirit refused to fly from his lacerated flesh. A mourning dove appeared, and he flung himself on the frozen ground before her. "Oh, my daughter," he whispered, his teeth in the dirt. "Fly away."

A certain mockingbird woke Iris each morning and lullabied Boy Found each night. Iris knew it was the same one because it always perched just outside her bedroom window, in the red cedar, and didn't fly away even when she walked right up close. It was the color of storm clouds, with only a streak here and there of startling white and a few fine stripes of black on its feathers.

Boy Found grew up with its song and accepted its constant presence without question, just as he accepted the other miracles that daily enfolded his awakening self: the sweetness of the star jasmines in his nostrils, the dance of the willows high above his head, the water-music of the river down the hill, the flick of tall green grasses on his skin and their fragrant crunch beneath his feet as he ran through the long meadow, his mother always close behind.

Iris kept different memories of those years in the woods. She remembered her panic when the side of venison, hung on the kitchen wall by W. B., was carved up, slice by slice, until it was gone. She remembered tiptoeing into the meadow to shoot a rabbit, as she'd seen Hattie do. Iris shot it dead finally, on the fourth try. It had screamed like a child. Screamed and screamed. And then stopped.

She remembered trying to skin it, holding on to the long ears and peeling back the fur like she was peeling a piece of fruit, but finding that pink-veined flesh, tender as infancy and still warm, peppered with buckshot. She boiled the water, but couldn't bear to drop the animal in, couldn't bear the thought of boiling that pink flesh until it turned gray and let go of its bones, couldn't bear the thought of actually stabbing that boiled flesh with a fork, and bringing it to her lips, and opening her mouth, and chewing. And swallowing.

So she wrapped it, ears and all, in a flour sack and ran out into the night, past the red cedar, past the lindens, past even the sycamores. She thought of burying it somewhere, but threw it instead, threw it with all her strength as far as she could from her tidy home, her hungry son, her pot of boiling water. She had hoped the white bundle would arc and fly in the black sky like a shooting star. But her arm was not good, and it just plopped to the earth, like a pile of dead meat and bloody bones, like just what it was, not two yards from her feet. She ran home and scrubbed her hands with lye soap and lots of hot water from the boiling pot. Then she nursed Boy Found, tearfully, for he was growing so big and needing so much. And she went to bed without eating at all.

Food remained the main problem for the first few weeks. Otherwise, they were quite comfortable. Iris chose for their bedroom a well-lighted room in the front of the rambling cabin; it had a brightly woven rag rug and a real down mattress on the floor. She draped both the rug and the mattress over the strong branches of an oak, then beat them in the fresh spring air until no trace of dust or Mildred remained. She attacked the corners of the room with the split broom she found in the kitchen, then scrubbed the cottonwood floor with a sudsy brush and with an energy that made the soft, cottony fibers stand up in a somewhat more prickly fashion than she had intended. But at least it was bug-free and clean enough for Boy Found to crawl on, and Iris was proud of her accomplishment until she realized that the crawling Boy Found would not stay in one room, nor did he have any interest in cleanliness, nor did he have any special aversion to bugs, not even to popping them into his mouth.

She cleaned up the other rooms too, even though she hardly ever entered most of them. She rummaged through the basement and found, besides the shoulder-high stacks of neatly folded, unwearable garments, a full cupboard of dried berries, jerkies, and put-up pickles. She also found (under the pile of extra grass-filled mattresses for guests, under the dusty bolts of yellow muslin, of sky blue gingham, of—and here her hand flew to her heart—burgundy velvet!) three big sacks of flour, four of cornmeal, a tin of lard, and enough red beans to last a lifetime. She and Boy Found would be fine. They would be fine all by themselves.

Early one summer morning, a whistle sounded that made Iris sit straight up in bed. It was not the mockingbird. It was not any of the birds that nested in her trees or in her rafters or under the tall bluestem grasses of her meadows, for she had learned their calls by heart.

This whistle was low and ragged, like wind blowing through whiskers. She dressed quickly and placed blankets all around the sleeping Boy Found so he wouldn't roll off the mattress. Then she took the shotgun from where it stood in the corner and set out to investigate. Squinting into the sun, Iris saw three figures in buckskin climbing up the hill to her cabin. They were dragging a canoe behind them filled with something that overflowed its edges. She squinted harder to see what they carried and by the time she figured out that it was pelts, mostly beaver from what she could see, the three figures had stopped climbing and were looking up at her. "Where's W. B.?" one of them hollered.

Iris thought about hollering back, but she'd never done that before, and besides, the answer was too long. She hitched up her skirts and started down the hill to speak with them, but stopped again when she saw the men backing up.

The one with the coonskin hat held up his right hand. "Stay right there, ma'am," he said. He pointed to his traveling companions each in turn. "Glen here, and this here Elgin, are workin' on a fever. W. B. give us food sometimes when we pass through. We thought he might have medicine." Iris moved to approach, but he held up his hand again. "If W. B. be gone, then we'll be moving along. Don't want to make no woman sick. Couldn't have that on my conscience."

Iris pushed through the columbine and thistle despite his protests. "Let me see them," she said.

"No, ma'am, I don't shoot no does and I don't hurt no women."

Iris studied the young men and saw up close their glassy eyes, their trembling hands. "Get them up the hill," she told the coonskin hat. "I'll ready their beds and put water on to boil."

She ran up ahead, wondering as she ran what she would do with the water when it boiled. Tea, she supposed. Sick people like tea. She shook the mattresses in the large room where Lem and his little brother used to sleep, then covered them with fresh tablecloths since she had not yet discovered where the Gruvers had kept the bed linens. She placed a pitcher of water and rags by each bed, so that when the two sweating men hobbled into the room all Coonskin had to do was to help them out of their dirty buckskins and boots and onto the soft mattresses.

"Thank you, ma'am," they both said when she bathed their hairy faces with the cool water, and she felt a little chill of recollected joy when they said it. It reminded her of when she was little, and dressed her dollies, and fussed over their bonnets. These men were obedient like her dollies, and grateful, and still. She could care for them and they would let her. Elgin was sweating hard, but Glen had the shakes so bad his teeth were chattering.

"Better burn it out," Coonskin said. "I'll get some pelts."

"Wait," Iris said. Those pelts would be crawling with fleas. "Come with me."

She led him downstairs and had him help her carry the stacks of misshapen woolen garments up from the basement. She quickly tacked the pieces together with yarn, just enough to keep them from slipping off her shivering patients, and wondered if poor, raving Mildred would have approved of these crazy patchwork coverlets. The patches were large and lopsided; pieced together they appeared to be fashioned from a giant needle in a giant's clumsy hand. Coonskin took off his hat when they were finished and rubbed his hairy cheek. "Do I hear a bairn?" he asked Iris.

Iris was considering how to answer such a peculiar question when she heard Boy Found. "I have to get my baby," she told the now hatless Coonskin. "Sit between them and put the cool rags on their faces," she instructed him, "like this."

He jabbed at his friend's faces with the rags, then grinned. "I love bairns," he called after her.

When Iris returned with Boy Found in her arms, Coonskin was enthusiastically slopping water all over the men's faces. Then he looked up.

"That's too wet," she told him. "You're getting their beds all wet."

"What's that?" he demanded.

"I said you're getting their . . ."

"No," he said, dropping the rags on the floor and rising to his feet. "I mean what is that?" He was pointing at Boy Found.

Iris frowned and stooped to retrieve the rags. "He is my son," she said.

The trapper chewed on his lower lip, then turned and stared out the window for a long time. "Mighty pretty country," he said sadly. And then he said, softer and more slowly, "I thought you was a good woman."

Iris carried Boy Found out and shut the door firmly behind them. She found her butcher knife and put it in her apron, then stood over the boiling water and tried to figure what to do with it. She decided that barley broth would help the men get their strength back quicker than tea, and quicker out of her house. Biscuits for Coonskin, she decided. Huge and heavy biscuits. She measured the baking powder and pounded in the flour. Heavy, *pound pound,* and, *pound,* filling. Let him see what it feels like to tramp through life with a load in his belly.

Boy Found played at her feet with wooden spoons while the barley brewed and the biscuits baked. "Hot," she said when he reached for the stove. "Sharp," she said when he reached for the knives. "Sorry," she said when he cried with frustration. But it was a dangerous world.

Coonskin dragged his stiff sleeve across his mouth and succeeded in burying the biscuit crumbs even deeper in his beard. He had managed to choke down five biscuits in succession, then poured in a quart of apple cider as chaser and belched the sustained, richly articulated belch of a contented man. "Name's Stewey," he said, after. "And I haven't et biscuits like that in more 'n six months." He paused to let another belch, this one half as long as the first, escape. "Thank you kindly, ma'am."

"My name is Mrs. Fane," Iris said. She was holding Glen's head with one hand and spooning in the broth with the other. "See what I'm doing?" she asked Stewey without looking at him. "Do the same for the other."

He went to his task silently, clumsily, and Iris sat with her back to him. Boy Found pulled himself up her skirt and banged on her knee with the wooden spoon he still held.

"Mrs. Fane?" Stewey began. "I shouldn't have spoke . . ."

"It's all right," Iris said. She told him the story of the Gruvers and how she came to be living there, but that was all he had a right to know. She turned her back to him again. It was hard enough to piece together for herself the crazy pieces of events that led her to this place—a Virginian widow raising an Indian child alone in the wilderness, nursing typhoid patients back to health, conversing with this closed-minded and repulsive trapper who, God willing, would be gone soon—she felt herself unraveling. She had neither the will nor the patience to stitch it all together for somebody else.

Glen gagged on a bit of barley and vomited on her apron and on Boy Found's hair. Iris was ready to put her dollies away then, away in the trunk with the latch snapped shut. But Glen, she saw when more of the trail came off on her rag, was just a boy. And when she came back from the river, having rinsed her apron and Boy Found's hair until both were clean and cold, and found Glen weeping in the small bed with embarrassment and misery, she said all right. She would tend to those boys, and she would care for them, and she would bring them back to life. And Stewey could stay and help or he could go straight to hell.

Isabella's mother smiled when her young daughter finally lay her black curls down on the white pillow. *"Je t'aime,"* she said as she kissed Isabella goodnight. *"Je t'aime toujours."* Isabella tucked the eiderdown comforters about her own daughters' feet. *"Je t'aime,"* she said to Iris. *"Je t'aime,"* she said to Iris's sisters as she blew out the candle. Iris washed Boy Found's sticky face and hands. She covered him in his gold and green and red blanket, then settled down beside him to watch him fall asleep. *"Je t'aime,"* she whispered as his long black lashes fluttered closed. *"Je t'aime,"* she whispered to me and Hugh and Henry later on, when the prairie sky softened and darkened and the stars sparked and crackled in the creamy black night.

"Je t'aime," said Boy Found when he learned to speak. And *"S'il te plait"* and *"Merci beaucoup."* My mother taught him to be courteous in two languages and she taught him, on long shady afternoons under the cool cottonwoods and on long snowy afternoons by the fireside, to read the Bible and Oren's Rousseau, and she taught him to write his letters and numbers. At first he wrote with white rocks on flat black boulders, but later, as Stewey brought more and more trappers and traders to Iris's cabin for lodging (and pressed payment out of them on her behalf), Boy Found wrote with real paper and pencils and ink pens brought from real cities. The lodgers paid with other goods too, like sugar, coffee, sheet music, store-bought bolts of muslin, and sometimes gold, and, once, oranges.

Iris was irritated at first at Stewey's presumption in bringing these people to her home. It had been so wonderful when Elgin and Glen and Stewey had finally packed up their gear and waved good-bye and left her and Boy Found blissfully alone. It was heaven to wake up again to the song of the mockingbird and to the sound of Boy Found breathing, and not to the morning man noises of throats clearing and spit hitting tin (or sometimes not) and hangover groans and growls.

In truth however, she had to admit to a certain fondness for Elgin and Glen, and sometimes Stewey even, once they were strong and clean and healthy again. They had, after all, nailed, sanded, and painted for her the outside walls of W. B's last, unfinished room addition. Fact is, if it weren't for them, her home would've stayed open and raggedy as a tipi. And they had hung another side of venison in her kitchen before they packed up and hit the trails again. No need for them to do that. They just did.

And besides, the lodgers Stewey brought back were not all that hard to accommodate, at least in small doses, once she got used to the idea. They brought with them news of the world, stories and songs, and most of them, like Elgin and Glen and Stewey, were gentle and weary men, more weary than naturally gentle, perhaps, but docile as dollies in their exhaustion and gratitude.

Iris came to count on at least one influx of visitors per season and she found that whenever she told Stewey of her hankerings, be it for paint, seed corn, Shakespeare, or a violin, miraculously those same goods arrived in the arms of her very next group of lodgers, as payment for services rendered.

Iris made a sign that read Boarding House: Roomers Welcome and nailed it to her front door. Stewey laughed at my mother when he saw it, since she was the one who was so all-fired set against the whole thing. Iris frowned at Stewey when he laughed, but she was glad, really, that he'd gotten her started in that whole boarding-house business. She graciously invited the newest smelly band of bedraggled men into her kitchen for hot onion soup and dumplings.

Boy Found grew along with her business. He watched his mother change from a shy young widow who accepted payment only when it was forced upon her to a woman who tallied her profits and noted her losses, who awakened to her own worth. Gradually, the soft hole of compassion in her heart was filled in with something more durable. The Life Stone, which fluctuated throughout most of this period between a pale, watery turquoise and a deep, aching blue, developed a new sheen, a new hardness; when Iris pulled it out from under her blouse it shot the sun's rays right back to the sky instead of absorbing them.

A certain Mr. Baldoon wandered through one spring, with a horde of Stewey's other hairy friends, and Iris was proud that she did not, despite his obvious despair over the recent death of his wife, allow any cotton-hearted nonsense on her part override the fact that he had resided at her premises and eaten her food for over three weeks without offering payment.

"I have been wanting a horse, Mr. Baldoon," she said to him just before the group moved on. "If you mean to lodge here again, I would consider a horse to be adequate payment for that stay and this one."

She wanted to add that a bay would be preferable, missing as she did her old mare from Virginia, but Mr. Baldoon's eyes were already so sad that the Life Stone quivered for a moment on her breast. She decided to say no more. He didn't appear to have heard her anyway. And besides, Boy Found was whining about lunch and pulling her back into the cabin. Iris shrugged as the party tramped away and she saw Stewey throw his arm around the delinquent guest. It was just a small business loss, after all, and one that she could certainly absorb.

Iris didn't worry anymore about Mr. Baldoon but she did worry about Boy Found. He was a perfect child—strong and smart. But the older he grew, it seemed, the more he needed her. It didn't feel right. Her own earliest memories were of running away from her mother, escaping her hugs, her warnings, her controls. But Boy Found was happiest when he was right by his mother's side, where he could see her and hear her—touch her arm or skirt. She was gratified at first that his small hand kept finding its way, unrequested, into her own. She was glad that he gazed into her eyes when he nursed, and patted the golden stone on her breast. She was glad that he trusted her, and believed her, and obeyed her when she told him to stay close so he wouldn't get lost.

But as he moved out of toddlerhood and learned to cut his own food and change his own clothes, as his short legs lengthened and grew muscular from running with his mother in the meadow, it began to concern her that he never ran alone.

The boarding-house men did little to reassure her. They made remarks about the way he clung to her skirts, and him already four years old, as Iris served the men their hominy and collard greens at the long table. They called him a "mama's boy" and worse things, right to his face, and although Iris ladled hot gravy into their laps when they said it, Boy Found didn't let go, even then.

The other thing about Boy Found that worried Iris, worried her awake at night and sometimes even in the brightest sun while he recited *Hamlet* to her in the garden, was the streak of wildness that danced around inside his body and shot out, at odd moments, like arrows. *"S'il te plait,"* Boy Found said to his mother, but saying it did not erase the danger in his raven black eyes. She watched it cover his face like a thundercloud when he studied the river. She saw it other times in the set of his shoulders when he bent to pick flowers. It was a tension, a wariness in his muscles, that made him look like a mountain lion poised to pounce. Or, thought Iris on bad days when she could almost see the Indian blood burning through his poor, tortured veins, it made him look like a bloodthirsty savage crouching in the shadows, just itching to bury an arrow in some naive white man's skull.

Boy Found was six years old before Iris got her horse. It was another bay, and Mr. Baldoon brought it. Mr. Baldoon looked younger than he had two years before, but there was still a sadness around his eyes that made the Life Stone quiver again.

"There you are, Mrs. Fane," he said as he handed her the reins. "I'll not have it said that Angus Dwelly Baldoon is a man who forgets his debts."

Iris stroked the bay's neck and mane. "She's beautiful," Iris said, and called for Boy Found to come look.

Boy Found ran over but didn't jump or squeal. He stopped short, then ran his fingers slowly along the muscled foreleg, across the belly, down the rump.

"The lad knows a horse when he sees one," said Mr. Baldoon.

Boy Found ripped his hand away as if he'd been stung. Then he turned slowly to face the speaker. Boy Found narrowed his eyes and clenched both fists, and if Iris had not been so absorbed in the mare she would have seen that the wildness was back. Mr. Baldoon saw it.

Beyond kneeling down to Boy Found's level, he spoke to the boy as if he were speaking to a man, gravely and respectfully. "The horse be fair payment," he said. "That is all she be." Boy Found's fists started to unclench. "No one is going to hurt your mother."

Iris almost let the reins slip through her fingers as she watched the strange exchange; Boy Found rarely said a word to the lodgers and never, ever, did he listen to them. Mr. Baldoon glanced up to see Iris's intent expression, then returned his gaze immediately to Boy Found. "I promise ye."

Boy Found folded his arms across his chest and studied the small bowlegged man. Then he backed up and pressed against his mother. *"Merci beaucoup,"* he said.

Mr. Baldoon climbed painfully to his feet, then unbuttoned his heavy leather coat and dropped it just outside the front door. "Do ye know what a Scotsman dreams about while tramping in the dirt and shiffering in the icy wind?"

Iris shook her head.

"He dreams of turnip stew, thick with barley, colored with carrots, and here and there a chunk of tender mutton, to give a man something to chew on." He pulled off his long muddy boots and dropped them just beside his coat. "Might there be anything of the sort in your warm kitchen, Mrs. Fane?"

Iris laughed and gestured him inside. "Go warm yourself, Mr. Baldoon. I have barley already boiling and am sure I can find some carrots and turnips. As for the mutton, unless you've seen sheep around these parts that I don't know about, you'll have to settle for dried buffalo."

Mr. Baldoon bowed from the waist.

"And you'll have to wait until I get my new horse settled."

Mr. Baldoon called to her against the wind as she led the horse away. "I will wait," he said.

Stewey showed up the next day with seven happy trappers. It was beaver they were after and beaver they had found. Hundreds of them. After they filled the canoes with the pelts, they stuffed pelts in their boots and hung them from their belts and piled them on their heads.

They barely even nodded at Mr. Baldoon as they pushed their way to the dinner table. They dumped their loads behind them and scrambled for seats.

Stewey smiled at his old friend at the other end of the table before he forked three boiled potatoes into his mouth. "Mrs. Fane," he called out, once his mouth was good and full. "Mighty fine harvest, wouldn't you say?"

Iris smiled and continued her way down the long table, pouring water from a pitcher into each man's mug.

"Don't know about you laddies," Stewey said, "but I ain't drinkin' water tonight!" He pulled a jug out from under his chair and held it up while the men cheered. "I'm celebratin'!"

"Pass it down here!" one of them shouted. "We're rich!" another one said. And to the accompaniment of hoots and bellows and knives pounding like war drums on the pitted oak table, the jug made its rounds from one bewhiskered pair of lips to another, losing much of its contents in transit and in the thick beards of those too impatient to aim.

"Gone!" said a burly German named Rolf, who stood up and threatened to bust the empty jug over someone's head if not granted his fair share.

"Now, now, friend," Stewey said appeasingly. He reached under the pile of pelts he kept still strapped to his chest and pulled out two more jugs. "For you, sir," he said, running and weaving his way to the far end of the table, personally delivering one full jug to the German.

They all waited silently until Rolf took the first swig, swallowed, and belched. Rolf smiled. *"Bravissimo!"* shouted a small Italian, then the knives started pounding and the jugs were handed round again. Voices grew louder, jokes cruder, and potatoes started flying overhead. The party had begun.

Only Mr. Baldoon did not join in. He was watching Iris. He was watching her rubbing her hands down her skirts and picking the potatoes up off the floor and catching the mugs of water as they fell and serving the carrots amid the wildly gesticulating arms of men telling stories.

"Mrs. Fane!" Stewey shouted. "Could you bring me your biscuits, please!"

Rolf choked and laughed and slammed his heavy fist on the table. "Yah! Biscuits!" he said, helpless with laughter and burying his head in his huge hairy arms.

Boy Found clung to his mother's skirt as she carried the biscuits to Stewey.

"Tell me, my perfect beauty, my lovely, my harp," Stewey began, "how do you like rich men?" Mr. Baldoon stood up at the other end of the table as Stewey pulled Iris into his lap. "We're not quite so dirty and nasty when we're rich, are we?"

"Leave her be," Mr. Baldoon said.

"I'll do what I want," Stewey said, reddening. "I'm the one who . . ."

"Leave her be," Mr. Baldoon said again.

"It's all right," Iris said to Mr. Baldoon. Then she elbowed Stewey in the ribs and tossed a mug of water in his face. "You're drunk," she told him as she pushed herself away.

Stewey jumped out of his chair, sputtering and stammering. "So I'm still not good enough for you, am I, Your Highness?" He started to bow but stumbled backward. His voice shook with anger. "Not even after all I've done for you—given you! None of that counts then, does it?" Stewey ran one shaking hand across his watering eyes, down his red face. "Iris," he said, reaching for her hand but missing it. "All them years, Iris?"

My mother's mouth went dry and she struggled to understand, to say the right thing. "Stewey, I didn't . . ."

"Damn right," Stewey said, straightening up and wiping his eyes again, this time on his stiff sleeves. He was staring right at Iris and the whiskers around his mouth were working hard to hold still.

"That's enough," said Mr. Baldoon.

"No it ain't," said Stewey. "'Tain't nearly enough." Stewey started slowly toward Mr. Baldoon; chips of dried mud fell from his boots with each heavy step. "I suppose you think that one stinkin' horse is goin' to buy you what I've given six stinkin' years to . . ."

"Sit down, Stewey."

"Hell! You think she's so perfect. Why that woman there . . ."

Mr. Baldoon grabbed Stewey by his shoulders. "I'm warning ye, Stewey. There's a wee boy in the room and I won't . . ."

Stewey pushed away. "You won't what! And besides," he said, looking around, "I don't see no boy in here. Nothing but that there half-breed bastard and he can jest run back to his thievin' tribe if he don't like . . ."

It was my father's fist that stopped him. Laid him out flat. Blood trickled from the corner of his mouth, and Iris hurried Boy Found out of the room. Mr. Baldoon ordered the other men to bed. Rolf grumbled and finished off his jug, then stumbled to a bedroom, where he laid claim to the softest mattress. The others, after satisfying themselves that both jugs were indeed completely dry, dragged themselves off without further protest and flopped down on the first stretch of empty floor that presented itself. Mr. Baldoon stayed to clean Stewey's wound. He covered Stewey with a couple of thick pelts, then left him to sleep it off.

The rest of the night was quiet, but Iris kept her eyes lowered next morning as she served the silent men their corn mush and coffee. Stewey pressed both palms to his temples to keep them from exploding and apologized to anyone who would listen for all he might have said or done the night before, although, as he explained, he really didn't have much recollection of it. Mr. Baldoon rose early and skipped breakfast altogether. He lit out for the barn, where he gave the bay a barrel of oats and brushed her coat with long, gentle strokes until it was soft and shiny. He felt worse even than Stewey because in all of the forty-three years he had lived, he had never before struck a human being.

There was another morning, later on, when Mr. Baldoon missed breakfast again. He'd been quiet that whole trip. Iris was disappointed; she'd come to count on him for company. He spoke to her of things the other men did not, and exercised her mare, and fed the fire, and sometimes he fed Boy Found too, when she was busy kneading dough. Iris was angry. When she checked his room she found his linens already pulled up taut and folded over. His pack was missing from the foot of his mattress, and she embarrassed herself by running to the window just to see if she might catch a glimpse of him before he was gone for good. But she saw only sunflowers, tall and wretched and dropping their petals, standing outside the window like tired sentinels, tired of standing and watching, tired of being on guard.

She thought of the bay, and of Mr. Baldoon's voice in the wind that first day as she led her to the stable. Now it was only the mockingbird that sang, "I will wait, I will wait," and the Life Stone hung on my mother's neck like a chunk of blue ice.

Iris remembered the heavy air of that damp morning—the morning after Mr. Baldoon hit Stewey, when the men bent over their coffee with glowering eyebrows, when Stewey's apologies fell like trees on the flat silence, when Mr. Baldoon's chair stood empty, all through breakfast, all through dinner. She remembered how the Life Stone sighed and softened that evening at the sound of Mr. Baldoon's footsteps, at the sight of his boots at the back door, at the scrape of his chair as he pulled it out and joined them at twilight for johnnycakes. She remembered how he toted his own dishes into the kitchen that evening, and how he helped her soap and rinse and dry, and how he thanked her for the meal then but even then didn't leave.

"You're most welcome," she told him, but he just shook his head. He took the dishrag away from her and held both her hands in his.

"I am beholden to ye," he said, "for more than that."

My mother braced herself. "What is it, Mr. Baldoon?"

"Stewey told me."

My mother pulled her hands away.

Mr. Baldoon smiled. "My sons," he said. "Elgin and Glen. The typhoid took their mother, but Stewey told me how you saved my boys." He carried a stack of dishes to the hutch and piled them carefully on the shelves.

Elgin and Glen. My mother clapped her hands together. Of course. She saw the resemblance then, around the eyes, the mouth. She smiled, remembering how Elgin had left her with that venison, all skinned and hung and ready. She remembered how Glen had fixed up that back room and planted for her a patch of hollyhocks. "Where are they now?"

Mr. Baldoon told Iris how Elgin had gone East and landed himself a job with the railroads. And he told her how Glen had given up on trapping and gone back to work their farm in Scottish Plains. Not because he had any particular love for farming, but because there was a certain Miss Mary MacNiven that he aimed to lay claim to.

"You can be real proud of your sons," she told Mr. Baldoon. "I can only hope Boy Found turns out half as well."

"I will help ye if I can," Mr. Baldoon said.

And my mother remembered feeling good when he said that, and for that moment safe. But now the Life Stone was icing up again and she gazed, shivering, at the failing sunflowers. Iris ran out into the wind, hoping it would stir her as it did the leaves of the cottonwoods. She didn't know where she was running—only that she should not stop.

She stopped at the open door of the barn.

Mr. Baldoon was braiding the mare's mane when she found him. His back was to the entrance and he was working gently, slowly, with thick, crooked fingers. Iris leaned against the door frame and held her breath as Mr. Baldoon sang to the mare in a low, flannel voice, in a language that Iris could not understand. She watched him shift his weight from one bowed leg to the other as he worked, in the same kind of rocking dance that mothers use to quiet infants. It sounded like music—this rhythmic shuffling sound of the straw beneath Mr. Baldoon's feet, this peaceful snorting of the mare as she took the alfalfa from Mr. Baldoon's hand, this muted rush of wind that still brushed against my mother's ankles but that could not now touch her face.

Iris wondered if this was what his first wife had seen in him—this impenetrable core of grace wrapped up in that aging, ragged package. She wondered if he had ever been young and strong and straight of limb, or if that had ever mattered.

The wind blew my mother's shadow into the barn and the bay whinnied; Mr. Baldoon turned around. My mother's dark silhouette in the bright door looked like a small moon eclipsing a vast sun. Mr. Baldoon did not smile or greet my mother, but only dusted his hands off on his trousers and went to her and stood before her and waited for her to speak.

"I thought you left," Iris said, and when Mr. Baldoon still did not respond she turned away from him to pull the Life Stone out from under her clothes where it was melting into hot tears that slid down between her breasts and dampened her blouse.

"Boy Found will be looking for me," she said, "and Stewey will be needing more coffee." But she only leaned toward the house, didn't move, just stood there, and Mr. Baldoon waited until she turned to him again, until she threaded her fingers into his own, until she pressed her arm up against his dusty sleeve and lay her cheek against his shoulder before he allowed his lips to brush against her hair and his voice to whisper in her ear, "I canna leave."

Stewey said he'd bring a preacher on his next trip. This meant (and this was yet another truth that I had to die to discover) that there was quite a lengthy honeymoon for my parents before the realities of marriage had to be dealt with. To my mother's credit, she wasted no time in anguishing over Eastern proprieties, but fell immediately to the task of being a real wife to my father with a willingness and enthusiasm that surprised even Mr. Baldoon. She obliged him in the hayloft, and out in the meadow, and even in the bedroom, while Boy Found was fishing or sent to pick berries.

It was the marriage part that gave my mother pause. It was the giving up of everything for a man, again, that made my mother point out the Indian pipe blossoms that were climbing up the hill or bend to examine one of the scattered vanilla orchids in the meadow whenever my father brought up the subject of marriage. It was the merging of the selves part, not the one into the other, but the she into the he, that frightened her. Marriage meant surrendering control, not only of her property, but of her destiny as well—both hers and Boy Found's—and that made her think of barbed arrows, of Holl Blankenship, of the Big Blue and of her forest green skirt in the icy water, pulling her under and not letting her kick. It was this that drove her out of Mr. Baldoon's warm arms and into the open air on so many moonlit nights, the Life Stone banging against her breast like a fist upon a door. It was the fear of it that made her pray, even loving Mr. Baldoon with a tenderness that made her sometimes weep, that Stewey would take his time in bringing that preacher back.

Mr. Baldoon didn't leave, and when Boy Found realized that he was not going to, he gradually eased his grip on his mother's apron. But he took out her butcher knife first.

Boy Found did not like the way my mother smiled for Mr. Baldoon. He did not like the way Mr. Baldoon put his arm around my mother's waist and he did not like being sent to pick berries. He sat for hours by the river and missed his dinner on several occasions just to make his white-lipped mother dash about and search for him and call out his name in a frightened, quivery voice.

"Your mother worries after ye," Mr. Baldoon told him one evening. "Don't ye be chasing off like that again."

The next day, Boy Found waited until Mr. Baldoon had gone out to find elk, and Iris had gone down to the river to do the washing, and then he crept into my mother's room and stabbed and slit her feather mattress with the butcher knife. He began at the top and employed the knife methodically, efficiently, aware of the weight of it in his hand, aware of the ease with which the fine tension in the fabric gave way to gaping wounds beneath the sharp point. He continued in this manner until the task was completed and even then he did not laugh or cry, but just ran far into the forest and plunged the knife deep into a cottonwood.

He stayed out all night and slept beneath some leaves. Mr. Baldoon found him next morning and carried him home, through the forest, through the meadow, through the vegetable garden, through the hollyhocks. The mockingbird was imitating a dove's song in the red cedar when they arrived and Iris was crumpled on the floor of her bedroom. She leapt to her feet when she saw them, her bowlegged Scotsman carrying her Indian son; she snatched Boy Found out of Mr. Baldoon's arms.

After she kissed and cried over him, after she checked for bruises and broken bones, after she rubbed his bloodless fingers warm again, she took him by the shoulders and stood him before her. "Boy Found," she began sternly. But his eyes were black as obsidian and the wildness, she saw, was back again.

Mr. Baldoon kneeled beside the boy and squeezed my mother's hand as he spoke. "What your mother wants to know," he said, "is what possessed ye?"

Boy Found turned his gaze to Mr. Baldoon and eyed him, silently. Then he spat in his face.

My mother gasped and dabbed at my father with her apron, but when Boy Found bolted for the door she caught him by the breeches and led him back to Mr. Baldoon. She unbuckled his belt and handed it to my father. "Now," she said to Boy Found. "You will apologize to Mr. Baldoon, and then you . . ."

My mother began to cry again. Mr. Baldoon accepted the belt and Boy Found froze. When they both turned to her with sad and sorry eyes she fled the room and they were left alone.

"I'm not sorry," Boy Found said.

"I can see that," said my father. He sighed and studied Boy Found silently, flicking the belt against his own palm.

"What are you going to do?" Boy Found asked in a softer voice.

Mr. Baldoon stood up and walked to the window. "I think ye know," he said.

Boy Found followed Mr. Baldoon with his eyes to the window but did not speak and did not move.

Mr. Baldoon held the belt behind his back and kept looking at the sunflowers. "Ye have hurt your mother sorely," he said. "Ye have stolen her knife and tore up her bed and made her sick with worry. And ye have insulted me." He turned back to the boy. "'Tis shameful behavior. It must have consequences. Aye?"

Boy Found said nothing, but didn't look away.

"Turn around, lad," Mr. Baldoon said.

Boy Found slowly complied, folding his arms across his chest, squeezing his eyes and mouth shut tight. Tighter. Nothing would escape his lips—not sound, not breath. Nothing. But then everything started to loosen. Couldn't help it. Even his tears were starting to slide then and he couldn't let Mr. Baldoon see that, he wouldn't, and then Mr. Baldoon put his hand on the boy's shoulder and told him to open his eyes and take a good long look at all he'd destroyed.

"See that?" Mr. Baldoon said, pointing at the bed. "That is where ye'll be spending the rest of your day, lad, and the next day too, if need be. Ye will gather up every solitary feather and ye will sit yourself here with a needle and thread until ye set it all to rights again." Mr. Baldoon tossed the belt on the lacerated mattress and reached for the doorknob. "And there'll be no more running off and making your mother cry, either, d'ye understand?"

Boy Found nodded. He waited until Mr. Baldoon had shut the door safely behind him then he snatched the belt from the bed, threaded it back into his pant loops and buckled it securely around his waist. It was when Boy Found crept out of the room to run away again, to get all the way gone this time, to run to some place where they could never, not in a hundred years, find him, that he saw Mr. Baldoon in the kitchen with Iris.

"There, there, woman," he said to her, kissing her hair. "You mothered my sons all the way back to life. 'Tis only fitting that I father yours." Boy Found watched Mr. Baldoon wipe away my mother's tears with his thick thumbs. "How could ye think I would hurt me own lad?"

It was then that Boy Found changed his mind and crept into the den instead of out the back door. He rummaged through his mother's sewing basket until he found a needle and the biggest spool of thread, and then he crept back into his mother's room and climbed onto his mother's bed and cried for a little while and then he started sewing.

The day Stewey brought the preacher back, Boy Found was following behind Mr. Baldoon in the fields, dropping seed corn in the new land he'd helped him clear. Iris was rocking on the porch, unraveling white yarn from one of Mildred's basement garments to make into a tiny sweater for the new little bairn who was due to arrive that spring.

Stewey paled when he saw my mother's condition, but nodded his head and went straight away to the fields to find Mr. Baldoon and to shake his hand.

"I do," Iris said when the preacher asked her, since there wasn't really much else she could say to that kind of a question. But she did, besides, and that made it easier. That, and the fact that Mr. Baldoon's child was prancing within her, and the fact that Boy Found charged every morning into the fields and threw his arms around Mr. Baldoon's legs.

Singing Bird stopped at a stream to gather more moss for her wounds. Moss stanched the bleeding, she found, better than magic, or lovers, or mothers. Cool moss from the edge of a stream where the water runs swiftly. Like braves do, she mused. Like handsome braves who pledge their love with burning eyes. Runs Swiftly was a name she would not soon forget. The memory of his words made her laugh as a mockingbird laughs, in short staccato notes without beginning or end. Without joy.

The Stone of Life was in her pouch, wrapped in leaves. It was still hot from the fires of the council and she dared not touch it. It was too much, this burden of blame. She could not go on. She could not bear this burden that was heaped on her like dirt on excrement. Heaped on her alone.

She saw Runs Swiftly again in the light of the campfire, and his shoulders were wide, his chest broad and smooth and golden in the flickering dance of the flames, his golden arms smooth ropes that tied her to the stake of him, his thighs hard and warm as gold against her own, and again Singing Bird wept, for the same dooming fire rose again between her legs and burned all the way up to her heart and shook her breath and made her strain and writhe with the pain of wanting again, of longing again for something not only forbidden and bad, but now lost forever.

It was too much to carry, that fire of the council, and that white-hot blade, and the white-hot hate of Black-Faced Bear as he carried that blade to her face, to her eye, and pressed it in, and dragged it across her youth, her hope, her future.

Singing Bird sat and stared into the swirling stream until the moss dried and shrunk on her face, until it fell off in chunks on her knees. She sat, still motionless, until the moon fell too. Three times it rose and fell before Singing Bird took what she needed from the water.

When she finally looked away, to the mountains, to the forest, her eyes were glassy and black as an arrowhead. She crawled along the shore until the feeling returned to her legs, then she waded far into the icy water. Sharp rocks cut through the soft leather of her moccasins and the swift current jabbed at the back of her legs like pointed sticks. She knelt down in the stream and ground her knees into the coarse sand.

Singing Bird held the Life Stone, safe in its pouch, deep in the freezing water. When her fingers were numb with cold she pulled it up again. Slowly, she opened the pouch, peeled the leaves off the cold stone, and held it up to the sun. "Too much," she said. "I will not accept it."

The stone warmed again in her fingers, then caught fire. She dropped it, and when it fell back in the water it hissed and cried. Bubbles rose to the surface and spit out steam. Then the Life Stone rose too. Singing Bird watched with horror as the Life Stone slowly ascended from the bottom of the clear stream, then leapt to the surface and danced on the ripples. In a panic she snatched it up and hurled it far downstream, with the current, away. She plunged her face into the water and willed herself to die. She watched the graceful undulations of the underwater grasses, of the shifting sands, of the tiny silvery fish who quickly grew accustomed to her presence and skirted about as before. She made herself focus on the colors and markings of the submerged boulders, as distraction from the growing pressure in her lungs, the burning, the realization that soon she would ascend, as the Life Stone had ascended, up and up, out of the water, out of the air, to a place without pain or love or scars, to a place where a heavenly father would lift her up and hold her safe, not knock her to the ground, or cut her, or shun her, as her earthly fathers had. And Singing Bird was smiling and watching the last bubbles of her life float out from between her dangling lips and up in front of her swollen eyes when she saw the Life Stone, glowing red and charging upstream through the water. She jerked her head up quick out of the way but the Life Stone flew to her hair and hung on with its teeth like a wolverine and that was when Singing Bird went mad.

Mad? All right. Awfully convenient, but plausible still. I guess I can see how all that blood and betrayal could well drive a body mad. I guess I can understand how the frustration and injustice of it all—all magic rocks aside—might swell in your heart and bloat up your belly and finally blow out your brains. And add to that the Life Stone, making you stay alive, awake, to see and breathe and feel and swallow every bit of it besides and yes, I confess I do believe that she may have gone mad.

But mad or not, there's no changing the fact that Singing Bird wounded a lot of people—a lot of innocents—and she used trickery and deceit and no one else could see that so no one ever knew. Except me. And maybe Boy Found.

It was Singing Bird, you must understand, who cawed lies in my husband's ear when he tried to forgive me. It was Singing Bird who swooped down and stole my little Dwelly away. And it was Singing Bird who sent her only son, sacrificed her only son, just to make sure as spit that I could never again run out on the plains, or wash my hair in a stream, or kiss my own husband, without first looking over my shoulder. For him.

Boy Found. Lost Man. My brother, protector. My ruin—because of her, I think, but the worst of it is that I am not innocent. For a long time I thought that I might be, but I'm not. Fact is, I'm not sure what happened. I can smell the steel, and hear the shot, and somewhere in the sky mixed up with all that blue was Dwelly's yellow hair and the cry and the three women. . . .

But I'm getting ahead of you now. I am sorry. Let's go back again. Let's try to line everything up again as if one moment led to the next. Let's lay it out all neat and logical, the way we like to see stories, the way we'd like to pretend Time moves, in one long line from beginning to end like wagon trails, or railroad tracks.

Time's not like that at all, you know. It is not like a trail, where each step moves you forward and the footprints you leave behind get dusted over and lost. There are no signposts that tell you when you are entering one town or leaving another. Time is more like a hutch full of china, or a drawer full of unmatched spoons, where moments can be stacked, staggered, rearranged, taken out for dinner parties, held up and admired and then washed and put away again, anytime you like.

Or maybe it's not. I don't know. Not for sure.

All I know for certain is that everyone was hurt and that it was my fault. Mine and Singing Bird's. And his. It was his fault too.

Singing Bird crouched by the river to push her baby out. Runs Swiftly had come to her in a dream and instructed her to give birth to their child in a cave. He told her that their son must be born in the dark, and be kept in the dark, or he would be doomed. In the dream, Singing Bird's face was still perfect and whole. Runs Swiftly gazed on her with eyes that burned like before, and he reached for her round breasts again and he kissed her so deeply that she lost herself and became him. And then she grew frightened and kicked her right foot, but it was his foot that moved. And when she screamed he bounded out of her, and took with him the parts of her that still clung to his flesh. And then he stood over her, her lips hanging from his chin, her heart dangling from his arm, and he wagged his bloody finger in her face and commanded her to have their child in a cave.

That was why, when the pains began, Singing Bird sought out the sun and followed it to its summer home, to where it swept across the sky like a prairie fire and leapt off the water as well, so that the light danced both above and below her as she labored, and there she grunted and swore and pushed her son out.

She wrapped him in a blanket of red and gold and green. She'd stolen it, along with a parfleche filled with cherry pemmican, along with a wooden plate and a horn spoon, along with the pearl white buckskin dress and pouch that had been set aside for the new bride of Black-Faced Bear, from her village while they slept.

She hadn't come to steal. She had come to find her mother, her father, to beg forgiveness, to throw herself at the feet of Chief One on the Wind, to eat with the dogs, do whatever she had to do to be taken back again. But her mother was not there and her father could not see her. He wore a heavy hide wrapped about him even though it was already the Moon of the Strawberry and the others had long before put away their winter robes. His face was smeared with blood and he spoke in a strange tongue, to himself only, and though he looked straight at his daughter he did not blink. Nor did the others when they saw her. Their steps neither slowed nor hastened. Their faces did not change nor did any words of greeting or scorn pass their lips. She reached out her arms to Kicked by a Deer, but even her childhood friend, little sister to Runs Swiftly, did not see her.

Singing Bird had become invisible.

Her arms became wings and flew up over her head. It did not matter then—her face, her sin. How could it matter if she was not really there? She was tempted to take what she needed right then in full daylight, in front of all of them. But she waited until nightfall, just in case the spell lifted all at once and exposed her deformity, and caused Kicked by a Deer to cry out in fear, or her father to strike her again. She took more supplies than she really needed, although she knew this to be sinful as well.

She chewed on the pemmican while her baby suckled. To distract herself from the afterbirth pains that gripped and clenched her belly as he nursed, Singing Bird shut her eyes and pretended that she could feel the grainy texture of the melted buffalo fat and marrow pressed against the roof of her mouth; she pretended that she still had a tongue with which to taste the sharp sweetness of the pulverized cherries. When the afterbirth was finally expelled, Singing Bird scraped off what she could of the blood and the soft flesh with her teeth, rubbed this on her baby's new skin for protection against cold and dark and men who deceive, and then she buried the membrane beneath a sycamore, with a prayer to the spirit of the earth that her sacrifice would one day be rewarded.

Singing Bird was not unprepared for the birth of this child. She had shortened many of her evening fires to set aside buffalo chips. These she had ground into a fine powder, silky as talc, to soothe her infant's tender skin. When she learned for certain that her own people had abandoned her, she had journeyed east, to find a good Bahanna, one who knew nothing of her past, one who would care for her ill-fated baby, one who would be kind enough and ignorant enough to bear for her the burden of the Stone of Life.

A wail of anguish swept through the bright canyon where Singing Bird labored. It ceased at the instant of her son's birth and Singing Bird cast her eyes directly to the sun in thanks. It was not Singing Bird who wailed, nor was it her infant. It was a Bahanna. It was the Bahanna who would answer all of her prayers.

When they had both regained their strength, Singing Bird climbed with her new son to the top of the canyon. She hid behind a tree and watched as a crowd of Bahannas gathered around one of the flock of white-topped wagons; their voices were angry and loud. She remained in this position all afternoon, all evening, all through the night, watching white people come and go and shout and sometimes kick the ground with tall, hard moccasins. She watched in particular one large female who climbed in and out of the wagon and appeared to be grieving.

It was late afternoon the next day before the people finally dispersed, and Singing Bird nursed her child again and dozed during the lull. She was awakened by the sound of crackling leaves, and of blade slicing earth, and of muffled tears. The large female was digging a hole near the base of an elm and placing within it something small, wrapped in a pale, shiny blanket. Then the large female covered the bundle with earth, waved her plump arm in the air, and hastened to the front of the wagon where she climbed up on top and snapped the horses into movement.

Unseen behind the clouds of new dust on the trail, Singing Bird unearthed the buried treasure and smiled. Thank you for saving my son, she said to the lifeless bundle. With gentle breaths she blew the dirt off the dead infant's face and then she wedged him high in a branch, taking care that he could not topple, to assure for him a swift and easy ascension to the heavens.

Sometimes, when her son cried out or needed to nurse, Singing Bird became uneasy. Then she would dart behind trees to satisfy him with her breast. Most of the time, however, she walked boldly behind the caravan of wagons with her papoose strapped to her back, secure in her own invisibility—proud, and somewhat vain of her new power.

When she realized that she could fly, when she saw that her arms were once again wings and that just by unfolding them she could rise in the air and soar, that's when Singing Bird decided it was time to compel the Bahanna, the sad, good Bahanna who had wailed at the loss of her babe, to come claim her new son.

So she covered the day with darkness and flew into the Bahanna's dreams and called to her to see, to see, to follow, to find, and then Singing Bird flew up to the heavens and flattered the spirit of the moon and promised it many favors in exchange for the safety of her new papoose and this good Bahanna.

Singing Bird wept and praised all the great spirits when she saw how perfectly her plan had unfolded, and she vowed to protect and to follow this kind, fierce Bahanna and to love her like a sister, and she was sorry, so sorry that she had to pass to this good woman the burden of the Life Stone, but it was stinging her then all over like nettles and she could no longer bear the pain.

So Singing Bird unfurled her feathery wings again and flew into the woman's wagon. She bequeathed to the woman her love and her curse, her son and her stone, and she bade both farewell with a bursting heart. Then she lifted the sickness from the woman's blood and when she flew out of the wagon again she was as light and as empty as air.

Boy Found and Mr. Baldoon were the only midwives present when Hugh was born. Boy Found's job was to dab at his mother's brow with a cool cloth and to let her squeeze his arm when the pains got bad. Mr. Baldoon was in charge of the actual delivery, including preparation and cleanup chores. All this he did expertly, having been through it already twice before. He counted the baking of Dundee cakes, traditional at Scottish births, as part of the preparation; he scooped the last one from the oven just as his wife had her first pain.

By the time Hugh was bathed and wrapped, Boy Found was hungry. So he and Mr. Baldoon sat next to Iris and the baby and stuffed themselves with Dundee cakes, then lay down on the floor and compared bellies.

"Mine's bigger," Boy Found said.

"Ye may be right," said Mr. Baldoon. He stretched his blunt fingers into something like a compass, then proceeded with mock seriousness to measure the circumference of first Boy Found's tight, round belly, and then his own. "*Mon Dieu!*" he exclaimed. "Yours is three times the size of mine. We'll have to pump some of those Dundee cakes out of there right away," he said, tickling Boy Found until the boy squealed and leapt on top of Mr. Baldoon, flying squirrel style, with the points of his small fingers unsheathed.

"You two hush!" Iris shouted in a whisper, so they crawled, still laughing, into the kitchen. When they crawled back again, too weak to laugh, Boy Found was amazed to find the baby still asleep.

"No thanks to either of you," Iris said.

"Well isn't that just like a bairn to miss out on everything," said Mr. Baldoon. Then he explained to Boy Found that bairns needed a lot of looking after, and that his mother would be counting on him to help. So Boy Found fetched talcum and pins for Iris, and he tagged along behind Mr. Baldoon as before, and his mother continued to tuck him into bed each night with a kiss and a *je t'aime* and the days passed more or less as they always had.

By the time Henry was born a year later, Boy Found began to take pleasure in holding the babies and burping them and jostling them when they cried. He learned that when he tired of their noises and demands, all he had to do was hand them back to his mother and she would kiss him and thank him for being such a help and then he was free to rejoin Mr. Baldoon again in the fields, or the barn, or the forest.

Boy Found was ten years old when I was born. Mr. Baldoon put me in Boy Found's arms as soon as I was swaddled, so his was the first face I saw. "This is your new sister," he told him, and then my father wept with joy and knelt by my mother's bed. "A wee little Iris," he whispered into my mother's ear.

But I was not to be another Iris. I was no rainbow goddess, no visionary. I was a loud, hungry baby who hated to sleep, hated to be tucked away in a room by myself without colors or faces or noise. "My heavens," my mother said to me often, in the middle of the night, "I surely was spoiled by your brothers."

Sometimes, after walking the halls and rocking me and trying every trick that had quieted my brothers, she would have to just lay me down and let me cry awhile, which upset the whole family, but especially Boy Found. After a few nights of that, Boy Found took it upon himself to get up and take me out of my crib and bounce me back to sleep. "You'll ruin her," my mother told him, but she didn't protest too much because she was so very tired and sleep was so sweet.

"She's really Boy Found's baby," my father bragged to Stewey. And then he'd demonstrate by lifting me from Boy Found's arms and making me howl, then replacing me and laughing when I cooed. It was a game that Boy Found took quite seriously.

He began spending less and less time in the fields just so he could stay inside and keep me happy. Iris frowned at the arrangement when she had time to think about it, but more often she was so caught up with scalding jars to preserve the cherries, blackberries, boxberries, chokeberries before the frost hit, or mopping up the mud those boys kept tracking in, or pulling Hugh out of the corn bin, or Henry out of a tree, that she was quietly grateful for the extra pair of hands. And besides, Boy Found was so gentle and tender with me that sometimes the Life Stone warmed on her breast just to see us together. It made her remember all the miracles that sometimes got buried in the endless piles of yams to be scrubbed and trousers to be mended and in the constant din of cries and shouts and childish questions that filled her days.

My name had been a matter of some concern. "It should start with an *I*," Iris said. "My mother would like that."

"How about Indian?" Boy Found suggested.

"Hmmmm," said my mother. "Inez, Ida, Ivy . . ."

"Irene, Imogene . . ." said my father.

"Indian," Boy Found said again.

"That's not a name," my mother told him. "India, maybe. That might work."

Then my father said that he thought he'd heard of someone with that name before, and my mother told him not to be silly, that she knew dozens of Indias back home and that it was a perfectly respectable name, and then they both looked at Boy Found and saw that he was happy with it too and that was that.

So I became India. The one in the box.

Boy Found loved me. He wanted me all to himself. Where he used to shrug off his little brothers' intrusions, he now grew impatient and angry. He once caught three-year-old Hugh trying to pick me up out of the cradle and told him that if he ever did that again that he would tie him to the red cedar and let the mockingbird peck out his eyes.

"Where did you get that kind of talk?" Iris asked Boy Found, when Hugh came crying. "What's gotten into you?"

"I don't care," Boy Found said. "And if anyone . . ." But here he stopped because Mr. Baldoon stormed into the room just then with his jaws clenched and his brows furrowed. Boy Found never had finished the plowing he'd set him to.

"What's this all about?" Sweat and dust ran down Mr. Baldoon's face. He narrowed his eyes and glared at Boy Found. "If anyone what, then what will ye do?"

"If anyone hurts her."

"No one would hurt her. Get back to your plowing."

"But if anyone did . . ."

Mr. Baldoon pulled a red handkerchief out of a back pocket and wiped his red face. "Sure, and what then, lad? Finish your thought, now that you've started it."

Boy Found gave me back to my mother, then stood in front of us and stared at his feet. "I'd kill 'im," he said.

"I see," said Mr. Baldoon. His blue eyes were bright with anger. "Now ye will finish your plowing, d'ye understand?" My father kept his eyes hard on Boy Found. "We will speak of this later," he called out as Boy Found stomped back to the fields. "Make no mistake about that."

I squirmed and kicked in my mother's arms. I was wailing like anything.

Mr. Baldoon called Boy Found into the study after supper that evening. He packed tobacco into his pipe, then held it up for Boy Found to light.

"Now what, I would like to know, was all that about this afternoon? No child of mine, not you, not Hugh, not Henry, not even little India, will ever be hurting or killing anyone. Not ever. I'll not have it. Do ye follow me, lad?" Mr. Baldoon leaned way forward as he spoke and hypnotized Boy Found with his thickly tangled eyebrows. "Speak up, then, I canna hear ye."

Boy Found nodded.

"Your mother worries about that kind of talk," he continued. "I do meself at times, I admit it." He puffed on his pipe and tried to find a way to explain how it is about love. How some kinds save and how other kinds strangle. He tried to find a way to reassure the boy, to comfort him, to let him know that love grew out of love just as surely as corn grew out of corn. That it took only tending, daily tending, to make it live. He wanted to show him that there was enough for all, that the more workers tended the corn, the larger would be the harvest, that a person, loved by many, could only become fuller, riper. More golden. Boy Found waited patiently as Mr. Baldoon puffed on his pipe, stood up, then sat down again.

How to explain these things to a nameless boy abandoned by his own mother? How to explain that he need not love so tightly to keep his beloved near? Mr. Baldoon dropped his heavy, square hand on the boy's head. "You air a good lad," he said, smiling.

He went to the window, thinking he might show the boy the vastness of the corn fields, of the forest behind them, of the sky behind that, thinking that the boy would understand then, without so many words. He motioned Boy Found to him, then gazed at the land, the endlessly fertile land, and opened his arms wide to the moon. "D'ye see that, then?" he asked Boy Found. "D'ye see then why ye canna love so hard and so tight and so small?"

Boy Found let his head rest against the cool, real glass in the study. He saw only corn. To be gathered, shucked, plowed under, and planted again. He tried to see what he should be seeing, but could not.

"Answer me, lad," said Mr. Baldoon, encircling the boy's thin arm with his thick fingers. "Or will I be needing to use that strap after all?"

Boy Found shook his head and narrowed his eyes, trying harder to see what he should.

"See there?" said Mr. Baldoon. "It grows and grows, if you let it." He tapped his pipe ashes out on the sill, then tried again. "But you canna love the way you do."

Boy Found stared hard at a single ear of green corn. The kernels were tiny orbs; they reminded him of his little sister's fingernails. "*Je vois,*" he said to Mr. Baldoon.

"There's a good lad," Mr. Baldoon said. He clapped him on the back and sent him off to say *bon soir* to his mother, his brothers, his sister.

Boy Found rubbed my baby fingernails back and forth across his lower lip. "I canna," he said. And when he slept he dreamt of a sky black with ravens. Their wings were hatchets. A huge white hand hovered overhead like a cloud, then swooped down and folded itself into a giant fist. "Stop," the fist said. But he didn't know what to stop and then the ravens all charged him at once, wings glinting and sharp in the smoke-filled air.

Boy Found stayed for as long as he could. My mother's voice at the piano kept him there, and my father's pipe and their walks in the forest, and the books and the rivers and the sweet star jasmine and I did too, I kept him there.

He stayed for nearly fourteen years but then he had to leave. My father saw it coming and tried to prepare my mother. Boy Found couldn't plow straight anymore, he told Iris. The lad's eyes kept drifting away from the lines of the earth. They went to the skies, to the hills; they followed the twisted flight of the mockingbird or sometimes they followed nothing and just grew darker, deeper, black as holes.

Many times Mr. Baldoon followed Boy Found in the fields and put his arm around his shoulders and tried to pull him back to them, but it was already too late. The boy would be leaving them, he told my mother. He saw Boy Found steal into my room one night and leave a package under my pillow. And it will be soon, he told her. So be ready.

Of course my mother had not been ready. And seven-year-old Hugh hated Boy Found forever for making our mother cry like that. She cried and cried and then she walked around like she was still asleep, sometimes forgetting to make our meals or wash our clothes, just as if she didn't even have any other children.

But Mr. Baldoon would step in then, and make for us cock-a-leekie soup and scones, or sometimes Clootie pudding, and he'd tell us stories of Scotland and of men who wore skirts, and then he'd dance a little jig just to make us all laugh. And when our mother found us like that, alive and silly and sitting in the kitchen, then she'd forget about Boy Found for a few minutes and remember us. And after a while Iris came back to us completely, and she stopped wandering in the high grasses, and then she only let herself cry that one last time, when she realized that her mockingbird had flown away too.

Elgin and Glen stood on either side of my mother, holding on to her elbows. "It happened so sudden," my mother said, shaking her head as if she still couldn't believe it. "His heart just gave out." Elgin had a thick black mustache and wore a fine new brown suit; from time to time he pulled a gold watch out of his chest pocket and glanced at the movement of its hands. Glen had grown somewhat portly, but his sky blue eyes were kind and happy behind the sadness of the day; his wife and four daughters wept quietly behind him.

I was standing between Jesse and Hugh as they lowered my father into the earth. The preacher was droning on about sin and salvation and some other nonsense when I felt both my husband and my brother stiffen at my sides. Hugh said "damn" and Jesse reached for his revolver; I looked up and saw it too.

It was an Indian, a male, and he was looking down on us from

Gonner's Cliff, from the other side of the river. He sat still and stiffly on a snorting, stamping pony. His face and arms were black as soot. Large feather roaches of gold and black fanned out like a sunrise from behind his head and shoulders. A quill breastplate, white as bones, shimmered across his brown chest. Fringed leather leggings covered his long legs and partly obscured the red and green and gold beading on his moccasins. In his right hand he held a tall feathered staff; attached to the top of it was the head of an eagle.

Hugh stared at the figure and ground his teeth. Jesse kept looking at the Indian, then at me, then back at the Indian again. When the lone figure on the cliff lifted his eagle staff, Jesse shoved me behind Hugh and whipped his revolver from its holster.

Stewey stole up behind us then and placed a hand on each of the men's shoulders. "Leave him be," he whispered. "He's here for Angus. That's all."

My mother never did see Boy Found nor any of the commotion. She was leaning against Glen and watching Elgin shovel dirt on top of her husband. Henry had gone to our mother's side, replacing Elgin at her left elbow. I didn't want to look away from my father, but I couldn't keep my eyes off the feathered man on the cliff. He was looking at me too, and that made both Hugh and Jesse real fidgety.

My sons, Brodie and Cam, had already forgotten why they were there and were tearing around like little redskins themselves. Jesse and I lit out after them before they ran into the forest and got themselves lost completely. Jesse gave Brodie a good whack on the backside when we finally caught up with them and by the time I got Brodie to stop his howling and Cameron to pay attention, my mother and all our guests were making their way back to the house. When I glanced up at the cliff again it was bleak and deserted as ever.

Iris told her guests it was a miracle, and it lifted her spirits a bit, that her mockingbird should fly back on the day of her husband's wake. She filled everyone's glass with either cider or ale, and together they cheered the bright chattering in the red cedar and drank to the return of the noisy bird.

There was a morning when I was four, when the mockingbird did not sing. I remembered it because the silence woke me up. First silence, clear and cold as water, and then my mother's low sobs, dripping from the morning like the melting icicles that were dripping from the eaves. I remembered pulling my pillow around my ears to stop the plopping sounds, and when I did my fingers brushed against something stiff and long and tied with yarn. I sat up and tugged at the end of the yarn and peeled back the crispy, yellowing paper. Inside was a huge feather, gold and black and gray, with a thick quill that ran straight up its center and did not bend.

I remembered all of that at my father's wake. I remembered also that I had never told anyone about the package I found under my pillow, just studied it awhile then hid it under my mattress. I wanted to keep it all for myself.

When I described the feather to Hugh, later on, without telling him that I had it, he said that it must have been from a real big bird, like a hawk, maybe, or maybe even an eagle. For nearly a month it became part of my nightly ritual. After I said my prayers to bless my mother and my father and my two big brothers and to please bring that other brother back to me and my mother, please, I would reach my stubby fingers underneath my mattress and grope around until I felt my feather and then I would say a special prayer to the enormous handsome bird that it must have been plucked from and beg him to forgive me for keeping it there in my room instead of searching out his poor incomplete body and poking it back in where it belonged.

But that only lasted until Henry showed me a cave where he said giant bears were hibernating, and then I forgot all about the feather. That is, until I saw that eagle staff on the day of my father's funeral.

Everyone was still drinking ale and cider and exchanging sentimental stories about Mr. Baldoon when I smiled and nodded my way through the crowds to get to my old bedroom. I had to see if the feather was really there or if I had just imagined the whole thing. Jesse and I took the east room once we got married; it was larger and had a wood stove, and kept me closer to the roar of the Big Blue. But all these extra stay-over guests meant that we would be moving back into this pink and ruffled room for a night or two. I had to find the feather before Jesse did. He would laugh if he found it, maybe toss it away. Maybe ask questions I just couldn't answer.

My mother was already kneeling on the floor when I arrived, with her hand beneath the old mattress. She raised her finger to her lips when she saw my surprise. "I think we'd better move this now," she said, and flashed me a smile like a wink as if I'd know what she meant. I knelt on the floor beside her, helped her lift the heavy mattress.

She smuggled it out just before Jesse burst in. He'd had quite a bit of ale already and his eyes were shining bright as his smile. "Been lookin' all over for you," he said, and then he put his hands under my arms and lifted me right off the ground. I felt like a rag doll dangling in the air but smiled down on him anyway as he kicked the door shut behind us. He set me down on the bed and brushed his lips along my collarbone, up my throat. Then he lay his head over my heart and stayed there for a long time. When he looked up at me again his eyes were bleary and frightened.

"I'm gonna get us off this place," he said. "I'm gonna get us somewheres of our own." I missed my father all of a sudden just then and started to cry. Jesse placed his large rough hands on either side of my head and kissed my eyes. "I promise," he told me.

Jesse and I used to run all the time. We ran till we were clean past the corn fields, clean past Mr. Baldoon and my hand-wringing mother, and then we really ran, racing through the spring fields of goldenrod and then through the gray-green grass of summer. We laughed when we ran because we couldn't help it, because running fast like that, running fast as flying but stuck with feet that keep needing the earth, with feet that kept hitting ground again just when we thought we had lifted them forever, was fun, funny, absurd. The best part about running with Jesse, the part that made it better than running with my brothers or running by myself was the laughing, and eventually it was the falling and the laughing, and later on the rolling, and then the kissing, the kissing, the kissing in the pussytoes, and in the sweet verbena, and in the morning glories.

Mr. Baldoon picked armloads of wild roses, and shooting stars, and heartsease, and sun-cups for my wedding. Iris stitched for me a white cotton gown covered almost all over with real French lace. She dabbed at her eyes a little during the ceremony but not so much as would be embarrassing, and my father gave me away as calmly as if he'd been leading hogs to the trough. I guess they'd gotten used to the idea of Jesse and me and had done all their crying before.

Even then, Jesse had wanted to move away. He said that if he was going to give up cowboying for me then I had to give up those blamed corn fields for him. He said he wanted us to have our own place. I said, yes of course Jesse I'll go, I'd love to. I told him that I didn't even like corn.

But we stayed on for a little while anyways, until Jesse could round up enough money to start us somewhere else. And that took longer than we expected, what with him never having farmed, or trapped, or mined, or having learned to do just about anything except for cowboying, and then with me getting pregnant right off with little Brodie, and after that Cameron, and what with everything else that happens, I found out, when you don't really mean it to. And so we stayed on, and Jesse learned nearly to fit in, and we might have stayed there forever if only Lost Man hadn't turned up right when he did.

When I found out they were missing, really, not in the barn or out in the fields with Hugh or down by the river, I prayed to the eagle again. I prayed to him as I screamed for help, as I cradled my huge heavy belly in my arms and ran, ran hollering to Brodie, to Cammie, to come home, come home this instant. I prayed to the eagle to spread his wings and soar, to search for them, to find them, please, to pick them please up please please God in his enormous talons and to bring my babies back to me.

The Life Stone bounced hard against the bones of my chest as I ran. It made sick thudding sounds, like apples falling off a tree. I screamed for help as I ran, but no one could hear me. Hugh was out threshing, Jesse was gone off again finding us our new home, and Henry had taken Iris into town with crates full of books for the new library.

I saddled the bony old bay and traced the winding river for miles. We zigzagged again across the meadows, the fields, in and out of the forest. A snake spooked the mare at the edge of the wild grasslands; I jerked her back on course, cruelly, for she was frightened and thirsty and grieving like me, and then we went on, picking our way through the tall and endless grasses with as much hope of finding Brodie and Cam as we had of touching the stars in the darkening sky.

There was just a sliver of a moon, but the night was warm and mild and I prayed to my eagle to spread his giant wings over my children as they slept. Then I slipped off the bay's sagging back and settled myself on the ground. The dusky smell of moist earth and crushed grass rose in my nostrils. Small sharp stones dug into my arms, my hips, my thighs. The

Life Stone fell around backward when I lay down my head; the chain tugged on my throat, and I wondered if the weight of it might strangle me as I slept.

When I closed my eyes the slender, swaying grasses stretched high overhead, higher than the trees, and waved their tiny fists at me in pure maliciousness. They had not forgotten how Jesse and I had used them as a shield against the eyes of the world, how we'd trampled their seedlings and rolled in their flowers and laughed and moaned and clutched at one another, never minding what we ripped out of the earth or intruded upon, never minding anything but our own need and pleasure. And this, then, was how they would have their revenge: They hid my babies from me. They wound their long tendrilly arms tight around Brodie and Cam and squeezed the breath right out of them, and then they sucked my little boys back down into the earth to make up for what Jesse and I had taken.

I woke up choking in the dust and blinking in the sun. The grass really did look taller. I sat up fast. It looked taller because I was still on the ground and because the sun was scooting up the sky and because the bay had wandered away and left me alone.

For a moment I worried I might never get up. The ground was alive with sharp pebbles and the baby inside me (babies, I found out later) was heavy and ready and dropping lower each day. I had to kneel first before I could stand, just like an old woman.

When I finally got to my feet, I brushed the dirt and grass off my dress and looked around. Something was kicking up dust, something like a horse or a buggy, way far down the road. Might be Jesse coming home to us again. He would find the boys. For certain he would find the boys, if only he were home. More likely it was Henry's carriage, bringing Iris back from town, and that would be fine too. The tall grasses clawed and scratched at me as I pushed my way into sighting distance; they tripped me outright when I tried to run.

I reached for my belly first, put both hands on it to make sure the baby was still kicking. There was no movement for the longest time; I made promises to God that I really meant to keep. And God heard me I guess because then, at last, a sharp jab in the ribs, and then another. I breathed again and almost smiled, but looked up just in time to see the buggy, for it was my mother's buggy and not Jesse's horse, head on up to the house without looking back.

"India," a voice said behind me. I whirled my head around without lifting my heavy belly off the ground. I saw first the dark hooves, then the beaded moccasins, then the eagle staff in his right hand. And in front of him on the pony, safe in the circle of his left arm, were Brodie and Cam.

"I found them *la-bàs,*" he said, gesturing with his staff to a distant part of the grass.

And before I could even begin to thank him, the boys started crying for me and wiggling out of his arms, and I got up quick that time, you can believe me, and ran to them before they tumbled right off. The Indian lowered them down to me, then fastened his gaze on the road.

The buggy was coming back. Henry and Iris must have talked to Hugh and figured out that we were missing. They were looking for us. And with Hugh at the whip they would be finding us soon.

Brodie and Cam had entwined their arms around my legs. They wouldn't be running away again for some time, I figured. "I am so grateful to you," I told the Indian then. "I know my family will want to thank you too. What's your name? How can we find you again?"

He didn't answer. Just kept staring at the approaching buggy, at its riders, at my mother. I waved at her and she waved back. Then she brought her hand sharply to her lap and kept it there. She saw him too. The Indian sat still as stone. Abruptly, he turned his pony and galloped away; he cut a swath in the sea of grass that closed up behind him like water.

When Jesse came back and found out what had happened to his little boys, I half expected him to dust their britches for them right then and there. But he wasn't angry. It took him a while before he got angry, and when he did it was not at the boys. He knelt down in front of them and cradled one towhead in each of his enormous hands, then crushed them to his chest and looked away from us, biting on his cracked lips. He carried them into bed and tucked them in so tightly they could barely wiggle their toes. Then he had his coffee in the kitchen with us and went on and on about how glad and grateful he was to have them back home safe and sound and how he didn't care who saved them just so long as they were safe.

The angry part he saved for later, for me, when we were alone in the bedroom. "I could have found them myself," he told me. He washed his face and hands in the basin with quick, fierce movements, splashing muddied water all over the bureau and the white lace doily. He let the water drip from his hair and his chin as he glared at me. "I should've been the one to save them," he said.

I nodded, because he was right. He loved us hard as a fist. He would rather have lost his right hand than have us go through all that. He could have found them and he should have been the one. But he wasn't there and so he didn't. The Indian did.

Boy Found followed Singing Bird, but he did not want to. He loved his father and his mother and his brothers and his little sister with the golden hair and he wanted to stay always in the ranging cabin with the many rooms and the perfumed flowers. But Singing Bird loved her people too; the long years away from them had blunted the edges of her fury and there was much her people could give her son—should give her son, since they had withheld it from her. The Bahannas could not give him all he needed. They could not even know all he needed.

Singing Bird flew into Boy Found's dreams. Search for your people, she sang to him while he slept. Follow the ways of the Men Among Men.

But I canna leave, Boy Found argued in his dreams and during the day when she followed him from task to task, pleading, demanding. His head ached when he awoke, and ached when he went to bed, and sometimes Boy Found shut his eyes and covered his ears to keep her words out. But Singing Bird was determined. She swooped down on him in the fields and mocked his arguments with her insistent song. She flew in circles around his head and steered him off course, trying to make him anger his white father, trying to make his white father drive him away.

But the white father did not grow angry and did not drive him away. So Singing Bird tried something else.

You will hurt them if you stay, she told him. Your father will die, and your mother will sink beneath the waters, and the little girl with golden hair will curse your name forever.

Boy Found struck out at the air with his fists and cried aloud in his sleep, I will not hurt them I will not. But you will, Singing Bird sang it lightly, like a refrain: You will, you will, if you remain.

His white mother let him sleep late the next morning and fretted, when he awoke, about his paleness and his trembling hands. She begged him to confide in her, to let her help, and when he didn't answer she turned away and dabbed at her eyes with her apron. There, you see, Singing Bird whispered in Boy Found's ear, you have hurt her already.

"I must at least leave something for them," Boy Found told Singing Bird. "So they will remember me."

"It is better if they don't," she told him.

"I will leave something for them," Boy Found said. He was angry, and the way his skin stretched itself across his face and pulled at his eyes and thinned his lips made Singing Bird think of Dark River and she became afraid. She flew straight up into the clouds then and stayed so long that Boy Found began to hope that she had flown away.

But then a feather fluttered down, the largest feather of the largest eagle. And when it floated, magically, into his own open palm, Boy Found closed his fingers around it and bade farewell to everything he loved.

He left his Bahanna clothes at the far edge of the river and plunged in. Streams of sunlight broke the water into tiny diamonds on his brown back and made him look like a sleek, silvery fish slicing through the churning liquid. He swam across where the current was the swiftest. He wanted the current to be strong enough to either carry him back or pull him under and hold him there forever. It made him angry that it did neither. His arms became powerful with grief and fear and rage; they stabbed and slashed at the water, and he took some comfort in the wounds he inflicted. Never again, Boy Found vowed as the river slapped him in the face and rolled him like a silvery stone into other silvery stones that banged into his belly and his back, never.

"That was the River of Manhood," Singing Bird told him when he dragged himself out on the opposite bank. She watched him give up all the river he had swallowed. "Now you are free," she told him when he finished. She handed him two golden armbands, a loincloth, and a necklace made of dewclaws. "Go forth and find your fathers."

Black-Faced Bear was the first man he saw when he wandered into camp. He was an ugly man with heavy jowls that flapped against his face each time he took a step. He walked as if he wanted to stamp out everything in his path. His wife followed behind him, uncertain whether to step in his huge footsteps or to risk his wrath by making her own. She glanced up when she saw Boy Found, but said nothing.

Chief One on the Wind had gone to join the Great Spirit. He had always meant to appoint Dark River as his successor, but Dark River had fallen off the edge of the World of Men and no longer commanded the respect of the people. Black-Faced Bear was the chief's only son and the logical heir, but he was an unkind man, lacking both judgment and compassion. It surprised only a few warriors, therefore, when Chief One on the Wind summoned Runs Swiftly to his side.

"You have redeemed yourself in the eyes of the people and of the Great Spirit," he told him. "You are a brave warrior with many marks on his coup stick—more even than Dark River had on his before the Long Night of Sorrows. You shall no longer be called Runs Swiftly. From now on you shall be known as Stands and Speaks. And you shall lead our people."

Black-Faced Bear had been very angry. He would not again enter his father's tipi, not even when his father called his name. So it was to be Stands and Speaks, the new chief, who would inhale the old man's dying breath.

Kicked by a Deer ran to her brother when Boy Found arrived. Chief Stands and Speaks left his tipi to investigate the stranger personally, for he loved to go out in the sunshine and he prided himself on facing all dangers squarely.

Singing Bird, he thought, when he saw Boy Found, and the shame still burned in his blood when he thought of her perfection and of her ruin. He wanted to drive the boy from his sight with sticks and sharp spears. He wanted to bear the boy aloft, on his own burdened shoulders, to his own carefully furnished tipi, and lay before him all the priceless gifts of guilt and love—the elk's teeth necklaces, the conch shells, the dancing bells—that he had shored up and guarded for Singing Bird alone and had never shown to anyone else.

Instead, Chief Stands and Speaks stood and spoke. "Who are you," he asked the boy, "and where do you come from?"

"I am no one," Boy Found said. "I was found beneath a tree, and since then have followed the flights of birds." He pointed at Singing Bird, now a red-eyed vireo, in a nearby sycamore. "I followed that one here," he said.

"I saw you—you see me—I saw you—so what?" the vireo sang to Chief Stands and Speaks.

The chief looked into the bird's eyes and his dark skin glowed umber. To cover his embarrassment he signaled to his wife, Carries Much, to bring food for their young visitor, and water to drink.

"We shall sit now," he said to Boy Found and to the gathering cloud of onlookers. "Eat," he said, when the food arrived. "You shall sleep with my family tonight and tomorrow we shall talk. You shall have a new name when I come to know you better."

Boy Found learned the ways of his people. He learned to hunt with bow and arrow instead of with the rifle his white father had used. He caught fish with spears or his bare hands instead of hook and line.

He saved a man's life. He found one of the Snake people, with his gray-eyed squaw, deep in the forest. His thigh had been slashed open while defending his squaw from a cougar, and when Boy Found saw him he was wild-eyed with fever.

"We can't go back," the man said to his squaw. "I won't let them take you."

But the gray-eyed woman just smiled sadly and helped Boy Found bathe the wound and bind it. Boy Found carried them both on his horse, theirs having bolted when the cougar pounced. He carried them all the way back to their camp, even though the Shoshone were not friends to the Men Among Men. When they arrived, the gray-eyed one thanked him with her eyes and pressed something small and round—a gold wedding band—into his hand before a hairy white man in buckskins led her away.

Boy Found wanted to be a true Man Among Men. He attended a Sun Dance and proved his worth and manhood by allowing Walks with a Limp, the medicine man, to stick wooden skewers through his upper chest and dangle him from the central pole of the sacred lodge. He fasted and denied himself water and stared at a dead bat and a buffalo horn and the skin of a kingfisher and other sacred objects, hoping to have a vision, to find the protective spirit that would be his, that would determine his future. He listened to Chief Stands and Speaks and did all he suggested. He closed his ears to Singing Bird when she mocked the words of the chief.

But Boy Found did not have a vision. Not even after Walks with a Limp shook the tribal rattle in front of his eyes, not even after he journeyed to the High Hill and offered up three fox pelts to the north wind and wedged sharp stones between his toes and rested on pebbles as he had been instructed. He looked to the sky but saw only white sun and gray leaves above him. He gazed into the water but saw only fish and snakes and hollow reeds.

"Do not despair," the chief told him. "The greatest visions are often the most difficult to see." Chief Stands and Speaks motioned to his second wife, Touched by the Enemy, to bring his flute. This he passed to Boy Found with the assurance that the music of his flute would call forth the Dream.

Boy Found walked into the night and passed by the tipi of Black-Faced Bear. The flap was open so he entered and stood to the right, waiting to be offered the seat of the guest. He was not the only guest that evening. Seven braves and six young squaws sat around the fire, honoring Little Flower. The girl's hair was loose and her body was painted red. She bent over the fire wrapped in a robe of soft doeskin. The smoke smelled of juniper and sweet grass and white sage; Little Flower rocked and fanned the smoke into her face, her hair. She opened her robe slightly and coaxed it inside, as if wishing to be bathed in the fragrant vapors, even in the presence of all her guests.

"My daughter is now a woman," Black-Faced Bear announced, as he had at regular intervals throughout the evening.

The guests nodded their collective approval. Boy Found could not help noticing the smooth curve of the girl's painted breast when she opened her robe to the smoke. Black-Faced Bear noted the direction of Boy Found's eye, as did his wife, who hurried to rewrap her daughter into modesty.

"Enough," Black-Faced Bear said, with too much emphasis. The shocked expressions on the faces of his guests, the anger in the eyes of his daughter, restored to him his manners. Slowly, politely, he lifted his pipe and began to clean it. His guests stood, nodded, and cast one more respectful glance at Little Flower. Then they filed out of the tipi.

Boy Found took the flute with him into the forest. He could not sleep that night in the same tipi with Carries Much and Touched by the Enemy.

He could not bear the way their women's bodies shot out warmth like flaming arrows that ricocheted off the poles of the tipi. He could not bear the thought of Chief Stands and Speaks watching over him all night, waiting for the Dream to show itself. Boy Found knew that no animal spirit was going to arrive to protect him. He had been both deserted and deserter; he was not worthy of a noble protective spirit. He also knew that even if he had been worthy, even if a spirit took pity on him and strove to reveal itself, Singing Bird would beat it off with her wings.

He sat down under the stars and tilted the flute to his lips. He blew a few thin, quivery strands of melody into the night air, then licked the edges of his mouth. Sweet. Something sweet and powdery coated the mouthpiece. Boy Found tasted it again. Perhaps it was this powder and not the music that would bring the Dream. He sent grateful thoughts to Chief Stands and Speaks and felt a smudgy softness in the breeze that was new to him, and good. He used his tongue to explore the flute, every crevice and plane of it, seeking more of the powder that made the moon spin and the stars dance before his eyes.

It's coming, he said, as his bones softened and melted into the earth. The grass was wet on his back. He smiled as a green-black beetle struggled up and over the mountain of his chest. It's coming, I can feel it coming, he said, and the bright stars swirled and blurred into the clouding night. The Vision was coming and it would be there soon. He had only to shut his eyes to see it clearly. He had only to surrender this one time, to shut his eyes to all that seemed. To trust, to dream, to surrender to that which really was, and he would be saved. Another green-black beetle crawled over his belly, another slipped and struggled over the sweat-drenched skin of his thigh, but Boy Found had already escaped to the other side of awareness and he neither saw nor felt the beetles.

Saved. The word burst from his lips in short, hot puffs. His breaths came faster, harder; small clouds of steam rose from his mouth into the cold air.

He dreamt of long dark hair, swinging free as the ferns that cascade down the waterfall. He dreamt of red breasts, and then of robins, of sparrows, of mockingbirds. . . . His breath stopped and he sat upright, clutching his throat, but didn't awaken. Not now, he commanded, and his sleeping anger choked him, wrestled him to the ground. Get away from me and let me dream in peace.

The grip on his throat gradually eased, and as his breathing became deeper, more regular, the pictures tiptoed in again and brushed against his eyelids like feathers. Soft pictures of ferns, of hair, of corn silk, of coral, of women humming, of milk, of mornings, of a rose stone that swung out from his white mother's neck like a pendulum as she leaned over him and whispered him awake.

Warm tears slid off the sides of his face and made him dream of slipping down hillsides. Of running down loose rocks, of slipping and falling. Of everyone seeing. Of trying to run to get away from their eyes, their smiles. Unable to move. Sinking in mud, but kicking.

Kicking. His white mother running to him, too small to lift him. Little Flower opening her robe again and smiling. His little sister with the yellow hair cocking her head to one side and frowning, angry with him for falling, for sinking. No sound. Already the mud had muted his voice. It was swallowing him whole, bite by bite. First the voice, then the legs, penis, arms, heart. The eyes would be the last. A small mercy. At least he could still have the Vision. Even now he still might.

Stay! he cried to his white mother with his eyes. She cried too but didn't hear. A flapping of wings, closer, louder. His white mother sinking beside him. The mud. A screeching sound in his ears. Little Flower approaching. Her tongue a live snake, exploring his face, his neck, his belly, every crevice and plane, his arms buried helpless at his sides, his buried penis rising, his buried longing rising, helpless, help, his buried groans vibrating up from his feet, shaking him, the earth, the mud, sticky, oozing, her mouth full on his, long and soft hard deep, her mouth, her mouth, can't breathe, can't leave, her mouth, his little sister watching, yellow cornsilk hair, *je t'aime,* head cocked to the side. Why? she asks, whywhywhywhy, a flapping of wings, of mockingbird wings, a bird's voice at his ear little sister crying white mother sinking bird's voice I told you so I told you shaking but it coming my vision mother now it coming her mouth convulsive waiting it coming please hurry the mud it coming sticky now here there there. There.

He awoke in a puddle. The rain had fallen most of the night. The drops were large. The first ones settled into muddy pools around Boy Found's legs and arms and head, and under the shallow cave of his back. The later drops splashed hard into these pools and splattered mud up on the tenderest parts of his bare flesh.

Boy Found was aware of the sticky wetness in his hair, on his back, between his thighs, long before he opened his eyes. He kept tracing and retracing the steps of his dream, hoping that somewhere within it his vision was waiting to be discovered. He kept his eyes closed because he was afraid that the soft scarlets of the sunrise, the greenness of the grass, the silver shimmer on the blue lake would blind him to the grayness, the brownness, of the wolf, the beaver, the buffalo that was somewhere surely lurking behind a tree, behind a boulder, grazing off to the side somewhere, subtly, nobly, somewhere in his dream.

He lay still on his back until the mud began to cake and dry on his skin. The sun was high and red behind his lids and still he lay motionless, thinking, searching through the pieces of his dream as if pawing through piles of kindling to find the one branch that was smooth and straight and hard enough to be carved into a spear. He was hunting for the sacred animal that would lift his dream out of the body and into the spirit. He was searching for something, anything, that would justify the excitement that had spilled out onto his thighs while he slept and even now whitened his legs in the sun, as being holy and sanctified.

He found nothing. Slowly he lifted his pounding head off the muddy ground and sat up. Mud clung to his neck, his back, his armpits. There were no visions in his dream, only women. There were no strong animals, save the mockingbird, and he already knew who she was and how great was the price of her protection. It had been a body dream, nothing more. The lake was deep and cold. Boy Found swam far into the center but took no pleasure or refreshment from it. He tried to wash the shame away along with the mud; instead he walked back to camp with new burdens added to the old. Chief Stands and Speaks would be disappointed in him, ashamed, maybe angry as well. Black-Faced Bear would smile when he heard. Little Flower might laugh.

Little Flower. Her name brought back the dream and Boy Found felt his blood rush again. He hurried into the next water hole and sat in the coolness to calm himself before facing the chief. He hadn't felt this sick and frightened since he was a little boy, when his new white father held that belt in his hand and Boy Found thought that he meant to use it. He looked up just in time to see a dark shape pierce the white sky and dart up, out of sight. It could have been anything—a goose, an eagle, a buzzard, a vision— but now it was gone. If only he could have really seen it, the way his white father had wanted him to see the fields of corn.

At length, finding nothing in the water hole but his own wavering face cut into concentric circles that kept moving outward but never quite reached the edge, he climbed out of the water, letting the sun and wind dry him as he walked.

Little Flower was gathering firewood at the edge of camp, but Boy Found pretended not to see her. He strode directly to the tipi of Chief Stands and Speaks to confess his failure and to face the consequences. The flap of the tipi was fastened, but Boy Found opened it, rudely, without announcing himself, and went right in.

Carries Much was still dressing and looked up indignantly at the intrusion. But her eyes softened when she recognized the intruder. "You are all right," she said. "My husband has been worried." She smoothed down her skirt and her hair, then hurried out to find the chief.

The tipi was large, the largest in camp, but not large enough to house the tempest that tossed and trampled Boy Found's thoughts. He would rather Carries Much had chided him for his rudeness. He would rather she had given him the opportunity to be a man, to speak to her angrily, to put her in her place, thus elevating his own. Her gentleness wounded him. It made him a boy again, clinging to the safety of his mother's skirts as dirty men ate her food and laughed loudly and dribbled whiskey down their hairy chins. He stopped the tears that burned in his eyes by hurling a spear into the doeskin robe that lay crumpled on the floor.

"What has happened?" Chief Stands and Speaks demanded. Boy Found thought of the mattress he had long ago slashed with a knife, of his white mother's tears, of his white father kneeling before him and asking him then, "What possessed ye?"

Chief Stands and Speaks waited for an answer but was not looking at the damaged doeskin. "Speak," he said, when Boy Found did not. "You do not look the same. Tell me what has happened."

Boy Found studied the man who always studied him so intently. The man had fed him, sheltered him, taught him the ways of the Men Among Men. He owed this man the truth, and were it not for the shame and sickness that twisted in his gut, would have given him that.

"Tell me," the chief demanded again. "Did you see it?"

A brown-and-white bird flew into the tipi and made frantic circles around their heads. Two black necklaces adorned its throat. "Kill-dee," it shrieked, as it flew round and round. "Kill-dee," it screamed as it crashed into the sides of the tipi, again and again, then fell on the ground. Its small chest rose and fell so quickly that it seemed to be vibrating.

As Chief Stands and Speaks bent to retrieve it, the bird hobbled to its spindly feet. Spreading its wings as if they were broken, it headed for the open flap of the tipi.

"Do not let your eyes deceive you," Chief Stands and Speaks told Boy Found. "This bird is not hurt. She pretends like this to lure predators from her young." The chief laughed and gently pushed the bird along with his foot. "On your way, little friend," he said. "I am not a wolf and you have no children here!"

The bird turned and flew at the chief's eyes. "There," he said, catching it with both hands while it continued to peck at his fingers. "That is enough." He was no longer laughing. He placed his thumbs over the two black bands and pressed.

"Do not!" Boy Found said sharply. The chief glared at the boy and ground his teeth at his impertinence. It was then that Boy Found saw something in the black wildness of the older man's eyes that he had missed before. "My father," he said, bowing to his chief.

Chief Stands and Speaks blinked and stiffened, then gently placed the bird outside the tipi and closed the flap. He lifted his arms to the apex of the tipi and offered thanks to the spirits who had allowed his son to find him. Then he sat cross-legged on the floor and offered the pipe to Boy Found. "My son." He spoke to Boy Found with his eyes, of the years they should have shared, of the woman they both loved, of regret and guilt and redemption. He forgot that Boy Found had never learned how to read the eyes of others. At length, he spoke aloud. "You have had a vision," he said finally.

Boy Found nodded, but fastened his gaze on the pipe. "I have seen it."

"Tell me now, my son. What did you see?"

Boy Found thought of the mud and the corn silk and the mouth and the red breast, but these were not speakable things. He thought of the dawn and the grass and the lake and of the dark shape that had pierced the sky. "I saw an eagle, Father." And when he saw how much this pleased the chief, he continued. "I had a vision of a golden eagle. His brilliance filled the sky. I watched him snare a cougar with his giant talons, and then he set it at my feet."

Chief Stands and Speaks clasped his hands together and started to chant.

Boy Found was riding a runaway horse. His face burned and he could barely speak. But the fire in his father's eyes was like a spear in his horse's rump; he was galloping at full speed, and whether his horse led him into an ambush or over a cliff was no more under his control than his futile quest for a vision had been. He couldn't stop and he couldn't turn back. So he continued.

"And then, Father," he said, "the remarkable part was this. The eagle soared to the earth and stood beside me. We walked together through the forest. All the beasts, great and small, stood aside as we passed."

Chief Stands and Speaks rocked back and forth with closed eyes and chanted his gratitude to the heavens. The eagle was the noblest of spirits, and for his own son to be granted that vision of all visions was an honor beyond his happiest dreams.

"You shall be known as Walks with Eagles," the chief said, "from this day forward." Father slapped son on the knee and indicated that he too should be offering up thanks. Boy Found complied, rocking and chanting beside his true father. He kept his own clasped hands hard against his forehead so that this man, who had denied him once, might not see that he was pretending. Just as his own mad mother—that necklaced bird—had been pretending.

He could not have the flap of his father's tipi closed against him again.

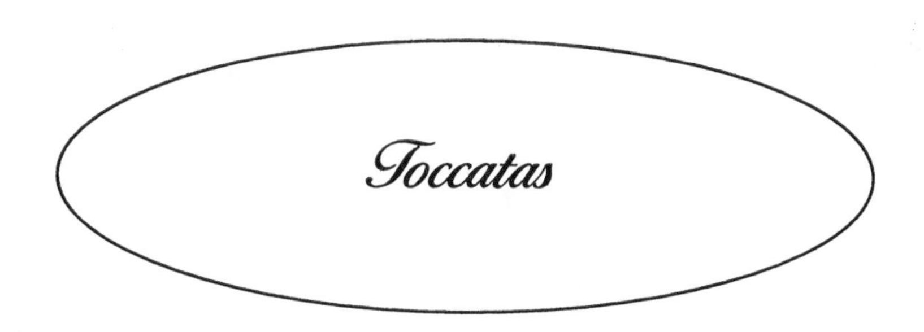

Toccatas

On my last night in my mother's house I finished crocheting the afghan. I'd started it months before just to see what it would become. I liked the ways the colors rubbed against each other and sparked or sighed or smiled as they grew in my fingers and spread out like paint on my lap. I also liked tying knots. I liked to pretend that each knot was a step forward, from nowhere to somewhere, from nothing to something. I liked to think that I could make that much happen, all by myself.

Jesse liked to watch me crochet. He was proud of my speed and of the way I made the hook flash in the candlelight. He told me I looked peaceful when I worked, like a real wife. Sometimes he sat at my feet when he said that, and helped me wind yarn into balls, so I had to believe that he meant it real nice.

I thought about old Mildred every time I unraveled one of her basement garments. She had some beautiful wools down there. Amethyst and kitten grays and blues as clear as periwinkle blossoms. They had to be pretty or I wouldn't use them—not with all that queerness attached.

My mother never heard from Mildred again, but Lem wrote once to say that his mother was doing better, spending ten minutes per day in the full sun, doctor's orders, but that his father was having some trouble in settling down. He said W. B. felt cramped up in a city room, and he acted kind of lost when he found out that doctoring others in their vices and afflictions was looked on as meddling in a real town. Lem enclosed a scrap of paper with a childish drawing of an Iris. "Love, Greta," it said on the bottom.

My mother kept it, along with a lock of hair from each of us and the newly minted Virginia coin that her father sent her, in a black lacquered box on the hearth. We were never allowed to touch the box, but now and then she took it down and held it open before our eyes, warning us to hold our breath as we looked, lest the baby curls blow clean away.

Up until that night, I crocheted only in odd snatches, waiting for the broth to boil in the big iron kettle, waiting for the tapioca to set, waiting for Jesse and the boys to wash up for supper, waiting for the pains to get harder, closer, so that those twins would finally be born.

I had a bit more time once they were born. Iris took over most of my chores herself for the first few weeks, and cooked for the whole crowd just like in the boarding-house days, just to keep me rested and full of milk for Colin and Kiel.

I had plenty of milk, all right. Sometimes, just in thinking of the twins, it would leak right through my clothes and onto the clean shirts I'd be folding. Sometimes, when Jesse was acting tough, I'd squirt it clear across the room right in his face, just to get him laughing again. For five whole months the twins got fatter and smilier, just like their pa, and I managed to crochet a full three feet of afghan between nursings and laundry and running after those two terrors, Brodie and Cam.

Then one night, Jesse came home from a riding trip and his eyes were shiny as a frozen pond. I would've figured that he'd been drinking again, except that his lips burned like a branding iron on my cheek. Iris led him away from the babies and made him lie down, and soon he was thrashing around on the mattress like a crazy man.

I never did get sick, which was lucky, Iris said, since then I could still nurse and care for the family. But sometimes I wished that I had caught the fever so I could be delirious too, so I could be crazy out of my head and wouldn't have to watch my babies shrink and wither before my very eyes and turn their parched little lips away from my bursting breasts.

The doctor said I did a fine job, that there wasn't anything I could've done any better. He said it was a miracle that I managed to pull my mother through, and Jesse and Hugh and Henry, and especially Brodie and Cam. He said it was a miracle, nothing less.

Jesse said it was his fault, the whole thing. He said that if he'd never gone into Lawrence to look for work he never would've eaten in that hotel or clicked glasses with those Walbach brothers who promised him a try in the saw mill and who, when he recollected it later on, looked kind of puny and pinched as if they were coming down with something even then.

I told him to stop thinking such nonsense. I told him that like as not he picked up that fever somewhere in our own county. I told him that it couldn't be helped and he couldn't have known. I told him time and time again. But he never did believe me.

Jesse wouldn't go to the funeral. I wished he had because I really needed him to lean against when they buried my babies. The Life Stone dragged on my neck like a lead sinker, and it was hard enough to hold my head up as it was, but without Jesse the pebbles kept on slipping out from under my feet and everyone's faces looked blurry and drowned.

I found him at home afterward, sitting between the two empty cradles. His head was hanging between his shoulders. I sat on my feet and tried to find his eyes. "Please, Jesse," I said to him. "Don't cry anymore."

He wasn't crying. When he looked at me I saw that the whites of his eyes were bright as new porcelain and the dark part was flat and gray as the head of a nail.

"Weren't my fault," he said.

"I know that, Jesse. I told you that."

"It was that Indian that done it."

You may think that remark took me by surprise, but fact was, I suspected the same thing. Singing Bird, with her long gray braids, her ugly face, still in a pearl white fringed dress even at her age, had been appearing to me for months before my family took ill. I thought I was seeing things the first few times—I saw her just out of the corner of my eye when I hung the laundry, when I seeded the chickens, when I slopped the hogs.

The routine went something like this: I'd wake up feeling wonderful, with hope springing and bouncing around inside me like growing babes. The Life Stone would be pink as peach blossoms, or a sunny yellow like buttercups. Then she'd appear to me, all of a sudden, for no good reason except to scare my happiness clean away. She'd sneak up behind, or slither around the sides, then *poof* away again the minute I whirled to face her. She shook the pretty colors clear out of the Life Stone every single time. Well, except for that one time when I swore at her and told her to stay the hell out of my life—that time she turned the Life Stone into a hunk of pure, lustrous gold. Real gold, which I should have gone and sold off right then if I'd had half a brain. Then she smiled at me with that blackened, twisted grin, as if to say you foolish girl, I am your life and you never will be shed of me.

"That Indian on the cliff," Jesse continued. "The one that . . ." He couldn't bring himself to say "saved the boys." "The one that watched your pa's funeral."

"But how could he?" I began.

"He put a hex on us or something," Jesse said. "I knew he would. Right from the start. Standing up there, looking down on us like we was prairie dogs, with that dead bird head on that stick. I knew he was up to something." Jesse pushed on the cradles as he stood up, and sent them both to rocking like crazy. "I shoulda shot him when I had the chance. Stewey shoulda let me shoot him."

I followed him to the window but he shook me off.

"Shit," he said, squinting his eyes to make out the outline of the cliff in the dusky sky. "Far as we know, he coulda kidnapped our boys hisself, then give them back to you just to make hisself look big."

I wound my arms around my husband and pressed myself against his back.

"It's all his doing," Jesse said, and he kept on staring out the window, but at least he let me lean against him, and after a while he turned around and held me too.

I put my hooks and yarns away after the funeral. The afghan was too heavy with memories and the colors were so sharp they cut. I kept up with the cooking and the cleaning and the caring for the boys, but beyond that I was weak as a newborn myself. It was a long time before I found the strength to lift the afghan again, or to look at it, or to actually tie another knot.

But then came moving day and everything was changing. For one thing, Henry and Hugh both took themselves silly brides, with nary a brain between the two of them. I wished they could have waited a little longer, at least until we were out of there; their giggles and petticoats cluttered up the house in ways that mama's lodgers never could have. So I didn't waste any tears in sad farewells to Ruby Nell or Lucille, I can tell you. I was anxious to move anyway, to get away from all the corn and grass and Gonner's Cliff. To get away from Singing Bird. My new in-laws only made it easier.

But if I was anxious, Jesse was downright jumpy. He fidgeted around like a little boy about to wet his britches every time he talked about it—the new house he was going to build just for us alone, the money he was going to make and the gowns he was going to buy me; the side crops he would tend and just a couple of cows and goats, enough to keep us in milk and cheese but not so many as to tie us down like slaves; the freedom we would have, the independence, the blessed peacefulness we would feel when we didn't have to worry about seeing that Indian every time we turned around.

In truth we hardly ever saw "that Indian," leastways not the one Jesse worried about. Unlike Singing Bird, who darted in and out of my life like a mosquito, the Indian from the cliff rarely showed himself except from a distance, and even then he looked more lonely than he did threatening, though I dared not say that to Jesse lest I start him in drinking again.

On the day before we were to begin our new life, the cat found a ball of yarn under the hoosier and started batting it around the kitchen. It was a pale coral color, like the inside of a shell, with flecks of gold running through that only showed up when the light hit just right, and although I couldn't imagine where it had come from, I stopped wrapping mugs then and ran to find my afghan. I was stronger by then. I lifted the unfinished afghan out of the sack I had buried it in and I gazed at it in the full sun.

The rest of the packing suffered, but I set Ruby Nell to helping Brodie and Cam with the tins, asked Lucille to finish up with the dishes, then I plopped myself in my mother's rocking chair on the porch and starting knotting like a soul possessed. I had to finish that afghan, to finish that one thing, before I left my mother's house. I had to work the coral into the rest of it, to make it fit in, to make the hard glint of gold rub up against the other colors even if the other colors pulled away. I had to make the knots close enough and tight enough to carry us, like a magic blanket, safe away to this distant, mythical land that existed inside my husband's head, where we could stand hand in hand and gaze far into the horizon without blinking.

I crocheted fast, faster, and the pull of the rough yarns in my hands wore raw lines into my fingers. I could hold out as long as the sun could, I decided, and I stabbed, looped, pulled, knotted, fast, faster, crocheting my family together, our journeys, our arrivals, as the sun slowly slipped down the blue bowl of the sky and orange and pink and then purple-gray washes slid down along behind.

I tied the last knot and the light was gone.

Inside, Iris was making a secret bundle. She tucked a real lace tablecloth that had been Isabella's into a linen pillowcase, along with her father's Virginia coin and a full set of napkins embroidered with bird-foot violets and yellow jessamine and Cherokee roses and coral honeysuckle. In the very heart of the bundle, wrapped in burgundy velvet and hidden under the napkins, was the eagle feather.

That part I didn't know about, or I might not have accepted it with such misty eyes and warm regret the next morning when she smuggled it into our wagon. I only knew for sure about the tablecloth, because I'd watched her from the doorway when she put that in. Knowing how much she loved it and remembering the Sunday dinners when she'd pulled it out and pressed it flat with the sad iron and placed smack on its center star the bright blue bowl piled high with oranges and berries, or Indian pinks, or almonds and walnuts for company, made me toss in my bed that night.

I dreamt that my mother laid the tablecloth in my arms, then cried because I could not carry it. At my touch it grew into a large and sticky web of lace. It sagged and drooped like too-warm taffy in my fingers and the harder I tried to hold on the faster it grew and lurched and tore at my hangnails as it plunged to the ground, and my mother kept crying, Don't let it touch the floor, don't let it, as if it were a flag. Then I couldn't move at all. Mama help me, I cried, *ma mère,* but when I looked up my mother had changed into someone with Singing Bird's face and Mildred's spider arms, and she was spinning her web around me and winding it tighter and tighter. She was laughing and I was crying until a tall woman in gray stepped forward and tore the webs away.

"Je t'aime," my mother said to Brodie and Cam before we left. She kneeled down on the floor and crushed them to her bony chest and even behind her closed lids the tears escaped and slid down over her sharpening cheekbones. *"Je t'aime, Grandmère,"* they said to her. They were too young to understand this good-bye, but the way their grandmother held them

made their chins quiver and their eyes large, and for a full three hours after we pulled away, they didn't fight or whine or even throw rocks at squirrels.

Iris and I were very careful. We didn't say too much or embrace too long. I pretended to be adjusting my bonnet as she slipped her secret bundle into the back of the wagon, wedging it between the barrels of beans and barley.

I waved to her as Jesse flicked the reins and the horses turned reluctantly away. Iris lifted her hand and stood in the doorway, alongside Hugh and Henry and their ginghamed wives. She pressed her lips together tightly but *Je t'aime,* her eyes said, and I was able to smile as I waved because I made myself think about the bright afghan my mother would find that night when she turned down her sheets to sleep.

Let me start again. Those weren't really the toccatas that I wanted you to touch. Please ignore the petty parts, about my brother's wives and about that cat. Ignore also the sad parts, about my babies—my twins. I didn't mean to touch all that, and you shouldn't have to either. What I wanted you to know is this: why I never did leave Jesse.

Because he carried my boots for me. That's why I never did leave Jesse. Because early one spring morning, after he'd moved us onto our own barren little plot of land and we'd already burned up through a scorching summer and scraped through a hungry, frozen winter and labored through the birth of little Jesse Jr., he rode out to town and brought back with him the good Mrs. Pinknell (smelling, as always, of turpentine and goose grease) to watch the children. He packed us a basket lunch of cold yams, pickled eggs, and apple cider, hitched up our horses, and rode with me clear out to Crazy Woman Creek.

He knew how I'd missed the blue water and the green that grew next to it. He knew how I'd missed the sound of a river when I woke and the cold, hard pull of it in my hair. There weren't many rivers out in those parts, not like there were back home. And none of them were big like the Big Blue, and none of them were close enough to dip your toes into whenever you needed to laugh.

So Jesse did all that for me and that is why I never did leave him, even after things got real bad. Because he lifted me off my horse and set me on the bank. Because he took the basket from my arms, and then the blanket, and then he unlaced my boots and took those from me too.

He carried them for me the whole way. I ran straight to the water and kept running, splashing, loving the water for soaking my skirts with blue, with cool. I looked back and saw Jesse way behind me on the bank but still following, watching me, carrying my boots, happy because I was happy. He carried my boots the whole way, just in case I might need them somewhere farther on.

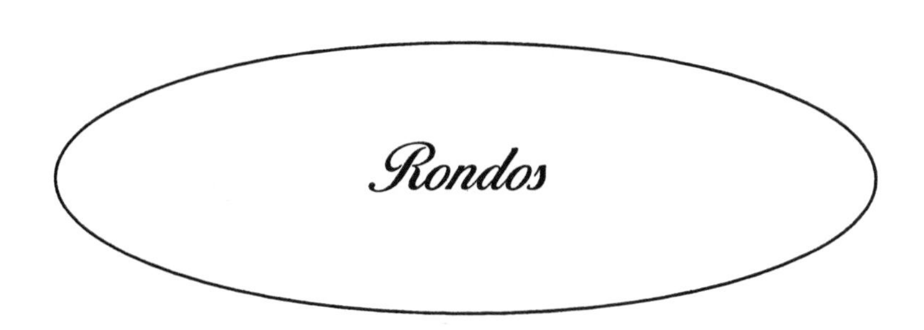

It was a difficult duty for Chief Stands and Speaks: to preside at the marriage feast of his only son to the daughter of his oldest enemy.

It was more difficult still, a difficulty verging on the impossible, for Black-Faced Bear to witness this blasphemous coupling. Boy Found had his mother's straight eyebrows, her leanness of face, her same pretty mouth. Black-Faced Bear had seen it straight off, just as the chief had. By rights, Boy Found should have been his own son, just as the chiefdom should have been his own birthright.

But Black-Faced Bear said nothing. He endured the long-winded speech by Chief Stands and Speaks recognizing Boy Found's miraculous vision. Officially renaming him Walks with Eagles. Acknowledging him as his rightful son and heir. Charging Little Flower to always conduct herself in the modest, helpful manner befitting the wife of a future chief. He endured the ceremonial presentation of tomahawk from father to son. He even endured the obligatory ceremonial gift of horses and buffalo robes from Stands and Speaks's household to his own.

What he could not endure was the thought of Little Flower moving out of his tipi and into the tipi of her new husband. Black-Faced Bear had not ended up with much in this world of men. His own black temper, he realized too late, had scared away from him not only the women, but the power and position that should have been his.

After Singing Bird disappeared, and her mother ran off, and her father went mad, Black-Faced Bear fell ill with fever. He had nearly fallen off the edge of the world himself, and when he regained himself he vowed to erase his black ways. He spent long weeks in the forest, fasting and praying for forgiveness, noting the arrangement of pebbles in shallow water, studying the movements of chipmunks and deer and all of the meeker animals.

When he returned to camp, he accepted potions from Walks with a Limp. The medicines made him feel happy and sleepy and calm. In time, he began looking at maidens again, and some of them, in time, returned his sly glances.

One of the maidens, Carries Much, allowed him to stand with her at the opening of her parents' tipi and throw his blanket over them and speak to her of dancing moons and singing skies. In time, Carries Much allowed him to touch her face and then, once, her breasts. To allow this to happen was a serious matter for Carries Much. If Black-Faced Bear were to discard her after this, her bride value would be greatly diminished. He vowed to care for her and to cherish her always. He gave his potions back to the medicine man, to ensure that his manhood could rise when necessary.

But then Singing Bird's lover returned. Runs Swiftly returned from exile and brought with him an oversized, unadorned parfleche filled with the dried meat of a bear he had tracked, slaughtered, and butchered himself. This he flung from his shoulder and lay before Chief One on the Wind, as an apology to his tribe. He was hailed as a great hunter and a modest young brave who had been wronged by an evil temptress.

And when this glorified outcast then threw himself at the feet of the chief and begged forgiveness, Carries Much gazed on the humbled creature softly and her eyes filled with tears.

That was when the black rage, so long suppressed and mollified and drugged into abeyance, returned to Black-Faced Bear. It began in his groin, and then boiled up through his blood until his face burned and his hands shook. Black-Faced Bear seized Carries Much roughly by the arm and yanked her into the woods.

There, hidden behind a thicket and the noise of the river, he hurled her to the ground and lifted her skirt. When she opened her mouth to speak he hit her in the jaw with his fist. After that she didn't struggle. He ordered her to close her eyes until he was finished. He didn't want her to watch him grunt and sweat and struggle. "Shut them!" he shouted and he slapped her hard, repeatedly, on the thigh, the buttocks, the face. "Shut them, my fawn-eyed love," he finally moaned in a slow, guttural snarl that made his words sound like a curse.

They set out for camp separately. Even if Carries Much did not tell his father, all was lost for Black-Faced Bear and he knew it. He saw it in the faces of his elders and in the glances of his peers. He saw it in the way the other maidens turned from him now, not with shyness but with shame, and with genuine fear. He saw it in his own face, where the blood still boiled then settled, permanently blackening and coarsening his already dark features, swelling his jowls and weighing down the corners of his mouth.

Carries Much, he learned later, had not returned to the tipi of her parents. She had wandered deeper into the forest. She vowed to keep her eyes closed, as Black-Faced Bear had commanded, until her body succumbed to either starvation or to a wild beast. Or until she could open them and gaze again upon a good and gracious world.

She was gone for seven days, and it was the crazy one, Dark River, who wouldn't stop searching, who finally found her. And it was the crazy one, Dark River, who wrapped her in his blood-stained robe and who, not having spoken to another living soul since the Long Night of Sadness, spoke to Carries Much and called her Daughter.

Dark River carried her home in his arms and laid her in the tipi of Chief One on the Wind. "She has come back to me," he told the chief. "I have been given another chance."

When Carries Much opened her eyes again, the chief himself knelt beside her. His eyes were good and gracious. He told her gently of Dark River's delusions.

"Then I shall go to him," she told the chief. Shame prevented her from returning to the tipi of her parents, and she wished never again to hear honeyed words of dancing moons or singing stars. "And I shall care for Dark River as if he were my father," she said.

The chief blessed her then and praised her strength and virtue. Like Dark River, the chief wished in his deepest heart to make amends for his treatment of their lost daughter, Singing Bird. "Your name shall be venerated by the Men Among Men," he told her. He touched her smooth face, still perfect and whole. "The shame is not yours," he said.

Black-Faced Bear remembered all this as he watched Little Flower pit a cherry for her new husband and place it on his tongue. Black-Faced Bear really had not been left with much in this world of men. Just a spiritless wife from a marriage ordered by his father; more horses and buffalo robes than he would need for the next several lives; and this child, this perfect daughter, this Little Flower, who was even now being torn from his heart and profaned by the gaze of the bastard son of the man whose penis Black-Faced Bear would have long ago severed if only his fool of a father hadn't forbade it.

Be careful. You are depending too much on these words and words can slither away and flatten themselves beneath rocks and lie in wait, and the prettiest ones—the iridescent corals, the shimmering golds, the emerald greens—are usually the most poisonous.

You would do better to note the way he padded around our soddy at night, or refused to grasp my husband's hand, or fingered the yellow hair of my own little Dwelly than to quote him the time he found me bawling near the pigpen because the hoppers got our little bit of wheat again along with my grandmother's lace tablecloth—the time he told me he would guard me with his life.

But I am confusing you. You were reading about Black-Faced Bear and here I am going on about Lost Man. They were both of them lost; I suppose that is the connection. But it wasn't my fault. Not for either one.

Except that it was partly my fault. I mean about Lost Man. I should have known by the way the dust smelled and by the way those sagebrush were squatting and leaning like little hunchbacks with outstretched arms and long greedy fingers that Jesse and I were going the wrong way. I should have known way back then, just three days west of my mother's real glass windows and Steinway piano, that we were headed into trouble.

Singing Bird knew. She planned the whole thing. I can see that now. I can see the bony white canopy of our wagon bouncing across the rocky plains. I can see the boys' heads popping in and out of the back opening like prairie dogs turning their nervous little snouts to the sun. I can see Jesse and me up front. Me with the broad calico bonnet I kept pushing back because I can't stand for anything to be blocking my view. Jesse's wide brown hands bunched around the reins of our team, steering us to our futures. Now and then one brown hand would uncrumple long enough to light on my shoulder or my bonnet or on my bare ankle just to make me smile and remember that we were finally starting out together, just then after all that time. Which is why I probably wouldn't have said anything even if I had known what was coming.

I would've smiled a lot more, though, made Jesse a lot happier, if Singing Bird hadn't been so hot on our trail. She followed us the whole way. It was easy for her at first. All she had to do was flit from cedar to cottonwood to willow. The trees were dense and she barely had to lift a feather, just step between the boughs with her scaly orange feet, and there she was. But after a while the spaces between trees got bigger until gradually there was more space than trees, and then finally there was only just space and hardly any trees at all. That must have made it tougher. Hiding herself in the scrub and the brush. Changing her shape and her song to keep me from getting suspicious.

Looking back, I can see that it must have been her wings, not the wind like Jesse said, that beat against the canvas every night. That was just to keep me from feeling altogether safe as I laid my head against my husband's chest. I remember also a sage hen that could not be caught. The boys tried first, and then I tried, and then even Jesse with his shotgun missed.

That was Singing Bird. And it was Singing Bird I heard cawing up in that tiny dwarfed maple in front of our new little sod hut. That was why I busted out crying when Jesse hitched our wagon to that maple. To think that I couldn't be free of her even in that jagged, angry country. It took me the better part of the evening to convince Jesse that it was not because our house was made of dirt that I cried.

In truth I loved our little soddy, at least at first. Before the rains came and dripped mud all over the yellow muslin bunting I was piecing together for the new baby. The soddy was a cool little refuge from the pounding sun, and I loved to think of Jesse thinking of us as he sliced and packed and smoothed and bricked us a home out of the earth itself.

First thing Brodie did was punch his fist through one of the greased paper windows, but it was warm yet and no one really cared. We unhooked the canvas canopy from our wagon and spread it over our new hard-mud floor. We unloaded what was left of the provisions, then sat Indian style on the canvas while we nibbled on jerky and our last tin of oysters. Cameron ran in circles while he ate. We rolled up extra trousers and tablecloths for makeshift pillows, then lay back and watched the stars bloom through the grassy cracks in the roof.

After the boys fell asleep Jesse and I rolled around on the floor, finding all the bumps that still needed smoothing, laughing at the sharp jabs of hip against rib, tasting, inhaling, devouring the rich aroma of earth along with each other. We were both new in a new life and it was paradise. I remember thinking that exactly. Paradise.

It wasn't until much later, after Lost Man found me, and said those things, and would not leave, that it occurred to me that holing up in all that dirt was kind of like being buried alive.

We were pretty well settled in before Jesse told me. I made little poufed curtains for the tiny windows out of a rose-colored petticoat that used to belong to my grandmother Isabella. Jesse found me a lovely smooth slab of gray rock for rolling out dough, and he helped me rig up a pantry of sorts by hanging a soft drape of white rabbit pelts (a gift from Stewey for our going away) in front of all the put-up pickles and preserves.

I was planting periwinkle seeds in the front yard when he told me about the Mennonites. They came from Russia, he told me, and they brought with them a new kind of wheat that was going to make us rich. Well, I perked up right away when he said that and I concentrated so hard on listening that I could barely hear what he said. But I remember his talking about the way this wheat grew, tough and tall, even on the parched and stingy plains. Red wheat. I was taken with the idea of scarlet crops waving all over our drab brown dirt. Sounds wonderful, I told him, and he got more excited by the minute. He'd worked out this deal, he told me (and that was why he'd been gone so much that past year—working out this deal to make us rich) with a man named Smokin' Joe Calloway.

Russian? I asked. No, of course he wasn't that, but he did wear solid gold spurs even when he wasn't riding, and he was in thick with the Mennonites, in with them on the bottom floor of this whole red wheat deal, and he'd been looking for someone just like Jesse to come along.

I sat back on my heels and forgot all about the periwinkles. Jesse's eyes were shining like mica, and I could almost feel the smooth caress of silk against my ribcage. I asked Jesse but how were we going to pay for a plow and a thresher and a pickax, and all the rest of it? At which point Jesse scooped me up and whooped and hollered and laughed and then brushed the dirt off my backside for me before setting me on my feet. He was brushing off my question too, I guess, because he never did answer, just told me don't you worry, gal. It'll only be for a little while and then we'll be rich!

Those were the days when I swallowed a lot. So I asked no more questions, just kissed his sweet, smiling face and took it all in with a gulp. I took it all in and I swallowed it down. Then I wiped my hands on my apron and ducked into our little dirt soddy. I squinted up at the grassy ceiling to watch the white-hot sun dangle dripping shimmers of light down into our home like a crystal chandelier.

There is a story for every star. Little Flower studied the sky and thought about that as she pulled on a woven sash looped around an oak and pushed her third son out into his father's world. This labor had been the easiest of the three, but even as she offered thanks to the spirits of the forests and the skies and the waters, she wept. She wept silently, as she had been trained, and felt deep shame for her ungrateful thoughts.

Her third son latched onto her breast quickly and easily, and she offered up thanks for this also. She was a fortunate woman, the most fortunate of women. She would one day be the wife of a chief, and she had given her husband three healthy sons. They were strong males; they would one day be honored warriors. They would have as many coups to their credit as had their esteemed grandfather, Chief Stands and Speaks, and their great-grandfather, Dark River.

Her husband, Walks with Eagles, had earned a few coups as well. Not as many as he should have, perhaps, but his beginnings had been strange and had made him distracted in battle. His strange beginnings had made him distracted in other areas as well. Little Flower's tears fell again. Even when she dressed for him in her softest buckskin and beads, she caught him sometimes looking up in the trees, as if he expected to see something there. Or sometimes late at night, when his arms enclosed her and his lips sealed hers, she felt him stiffen and catch his breath, as if listening for someone else.

But Walks with Eagles had been a good husband. He never struck her, as her father had her mother, and he praised her often for her skill in making garments, in making baskets, in making males. He helped her carve up meat for drying, cared tenderly for their sons, and many times assisted her in braiding her hair or in painting her face.

And so it perplexed Little Flower to find that her tears were endless, to find that her sorrow was as deep as it was silent. Something was not right with her husband. He was not really one of the Men Among Men, despite his blood and bearing. It shamed her, she realized, that he had never fulfilled his sacred obligation to kill the object of his vision, to bring home the head of the golden eagle, that its spirit might protect his home and his family.

She had spoken of it to her husband twice. Both times he had met her words with anger. The first time, he mocked her worry that he alone might not be man and spirit enough to protect her. The second time, he threw his bowl of boiled bull elk into the fire. She dared not speak of it again.

The baby had fallen asleep. Little Flower wrapped him in the soft doeskin she had prepared and then buried the afterbirth under an elm. A hawk appeared suddenly, swooping down through the trees with a whoosh of wind and feathered arms that nearly slapped Little Flower's face. When it dragged its talons across the new mound of earth, Little Flower cursed it and swung her fists at its head. Then she prayed frantically, guiltily, to every god she could think of. Forgive me, forgive me, she cried to the moon, to the stars, to the hawk, for she may have offended an important spirit and already brought doom to her innocent son.

Chief Stands and Speaks lay down and spoke of the matter to Carries Much. His son must complete his task, he told her. "I cannot live forever."

Carries Much traced small circles on her husband's forehead with the tips of her fingers. Then she smoothed out the crease between his eyes with firm, broad strokes of her thumbs. They slept now on the elk robe that had belonged to Dark River. "No man lives forever," she said, kneading the tight muscles in his neck with her strong fingers. "And you are right, my husband. He must do it himself." She wanted to add that he had helped his son too much already—that his favors, as chief, had weakened Walks with Eagles and had caused resentment within the tribe. But her husband needed rest, for he was no longer young. And besides, Stands and Speaks would take his son's side blindly, against anyone. Even her. So Carries Much rubbed his arms, shoulders, chest, and whispered in his ear, "Tomorrow you shall tell him," before she settled her head over his heart.

Walks with Eagles did not wish to go. He did not wish to profane the noblest of birds with his presence, nor did he wish to add the ashy sediment of murder to his already sullied conscience.

What he wished most of all was to back up ten years, re-enter his father's tipi, and say, Father, forgive me. I misspoke. I misunderstood your question. I was mistaken. For then, even if his father had scourged him with leathers, even if he had banished him from the tribe—even then he could have gone on being Boy Found, cut free but left whole, rather than being tied and cursed with a name that struck against his heart every time he heard it uttered.

But his father would have neither scourged nor banished him, Walks with Eagles knew, even if he had turned around and admitted the deception. His father would have been sickened and ashamed, but would have protected his son nonetheless. For his father was a good and honest man without any black secrets that pulled him from sleep.

"I will go," Walks with Eagles told his father. The people grumbled (as they smiled and cheered him on) that the chief's son should have fulfilled his obligations years before, and that despite the decrees and blessings and wishes of Chief Stands and Speaks, Walks with Eagles would never truly be one of the Men Among Men.

Walks with Eagles wanted to carry only a flask of water, a parfleche of pemmican, his bow, and a single arrow. He did not really wish to succeed; he wanted only to fly away. But at the last moment Little Flower came dashing at him with his coup staff and with a bundle she'd prepared. Courtesy demanded that he accept both.

"You will need this," she said, handing him the staff, "to record your triumphs. And this," she said, tying the bundle securely over the pony's rump into a kind of saddlebag, "you will want when you come home to us again."

A golden eagle displayed itself less than one day's ride from camp. It is as if he is hunting for me, thought Walks with Eagles. He became afraid. The bird hung in the air, midflight, wings outstretched, still as the great thunderbird itself. Its feathers threw gold flakes into the endless blue that surrounded them. Only when certain the man would follow did the eagle bow its shiny head and dive back into the clouds.

Walks with Eagles kicked his pony into a full gallop. They cut over hills and plowed through streams. He's calling to me, the Indian said to his pony. He wants me to follow him.

The eagle led him ever deeper into the forest. They flew through trees and time both. The undulating shadows of the forests made it difficult to know whether they were passing through day or night. Weariness could not catch them any more than they could catch the soaring eagle.

When the bird finally slowed, it was over a black and silent glen where the pines were either lying on their sides or posted like sentries with their branches curled down tight against their trunks. The fire had been a great one. Smoke and sorrow still hung in the air like echoes of a cry only recently stilled.

The white foam that bearded the pony's mouth glistened like a star in the unremitting darkness. Walks with Eagles felt a peculiar dizziness and wondered what sort of evil magic this was that could chase hunger and thirst from his human body.

The eagle hovered overhead, waiting, until Walks with Eagles slid off his suffering pony and led her to an ash-choked puddle of water. Then the bird floated down—it did not soar or dive—it floated softly, slowly, just as the eagle feather had floated down into Boy Found's open palm that long-ago afternoon in his white father's corn fields.

It floated with outstretched wings like an angel's until its spurred feet touched the earth, ten feet from where Walks with Eagles stood.

Walks with Eagles followed cautiously, with silent Indian steps, as the bird made its slow, stately way deeper into the ghost forest. He gained on the bird imperceptibly until his knee was within two yards of the predator's beak. A badger emerged from his hole then backed his way inside again, as if kowtowing to a superior. A doe stood aside and bowed her head. Walks with Eagles froze when he saw a great bear sniffing the path up ahead. But the eagle continued on, looking neither right nor left, and the great bear ambled away.

A burnt-out stump appeared before them. The eagle stood suddenly upon it, without even flapping his wings. "Now I have you," said Walks with Eagles, but he hoped that this was not true. He raised his bow and arrow slowly, expecting the eagle to dart away. He lifted the arrow to his eyes, amazed that the bird had not yet bolted, knowing that when it escaped, as it had to, in a great storm of wings, Walks with Eagles must either return to his people in shame, or die.

Still the eagle did not fly away. It did not move at all. It just puffed out its chest and gazed at Walks with Eagles with calm blue eyes.

"Stupid bird," said Walks with Eagles as he drew back the bow and aimed the arrow at its puffed-out chest.

"Go on," said the eagle kindly. More startling even than the sound of the familiar human voice in a feathered body were the blue eyes that gazed at Walks with Eagles. Mr. Baldoon's eyes.

"Father," whispered Walks with Eagles.

"Aye," said the bird. "For your father. 'Tis time, lad."

Walks with Eagles clenched his jaw. I canna, he wanted to say, but he knew better than to argue with Mr. Baldoon and besides, both of his fathers had willed it. Slowly, he pulled himself erect and slowly he drew the arrow back in the bow, slowly, with quivering arms. He cried out when the arrow leapt from his fingers.

His pony stood at his head, pawing at the barren ground, when Walks with Eagles awoke. At his feet lay a golden eagle, its talons curled tight, its open eyes the eyes of a dead eagle. The arrow had flown straight to its heart and had split its feathery chest.

The pines were still smoldering in the sunlight. The fire could not have been long extinguished before his father led him to this place. Walks with Eagles rose to his feet, unsteadily, then stumbled backward into a crater where the flames had consumed a tree down to its very roots.

So many of the pines were still standing. Even with their arms cut off, or their roots torched away. Some had kept their cores but lost their coverings. Others were hollow shells, still upright, but with their insides eaten out. The only sign of life or color for as far as he could see was the orangish meat exposed in the few fallen trees that had not been completely charred. The scene looked to Walks with Eagles like the aftermath of a bloody war party, where bellies were laid open and scalps ripped from their skulls by lances and hatchets.

Walks with Eagles looked purposely away from the great bird he had slain, but knelt at the corpse of a huge fallen pine. He pressed his palms hard into the blackened bark as if to massage life back into the giant.

Failing in this, he dragged his soot-covered hands across his face, arms, chest, and chanted, Father My Father My Father until he was altogether black with mourning, until his cries dried up in the white-hot sun, until the wind carried to him the distant sounds of women weeping.

He would follow the sounds to their source.

But first, he untied Little Flower's bundle and dressed himself in the fine leggings and beaded moccasins, the bone vest, the headpiece crowned with eagle feathers. He sliced the dead bird's head from its shoulders and impaled it on his coup stick.

Then Walks with Eagles mounted his pony and kicked it cruelly. He closed his eyes and rode hard through the dead forest, the clear streams, the endless oceans of golden grass. Mother, he said with his eyes to the sky, to the earth, to the water. Do not weep. I will come to you.

"My husband shall return to me today," Little Flower told Carries Much, as she had told her each day since the Moon of the Peach Tree Bloom.

"I am certain it is so," Carries Much replied, smiling gently. She hid her fears from Little Flower as she did from her husband. Chief Stands and Speaks was becoming one of the aged ones. He had seen more than fifty winters and his eyes grew sad when any man spoke of his son.

But the chief's waning strength and bulk seemed to fly straight to Carries Much. She grew larger every day. Her arms and waist thickened. Her breasts became two soft, full moons that pillowed scores of sleepy sons. Her hips spread out upon the earth like wide, soft cushions for the littlest daughters to sit upon while she told them the stories of their people.

"You are beautiful," Touched by the Enemy said to Carries Much. "Your compassion grows with your flesh." And in truth she prayed that Carries Much would grow even larger. Large enough to shield the chief from the ugly whispers that filled their camp.

The chief's son has been captured and is rotting in a Bahanna jail, was one of them. He has been eaten by the Great Bear, was another. He has deserted his wife and children and is hiding from his people, was the worst.

Walks with Eagles removed all his finery and tied it with his pony, with his staff, to a pine. Then he dove again into the River of Manhood. This time he swam from the opposite shore, hoping to retrace his steps, hoping to regain all that he had lost since Singing Bird had led him into that other world. He wanted to find his good white father still out in the fields, still wiping his red face with his red handkerchief—not trapped inside a box and hidden from the sky. He wanted to find his white mother young again, and smiling as she snapped green beans into a blue bowl.

Again he was pulled by the swift current and tossed with the silvery stones. Again he secretly wished that the water might drag him down and keep him there forever. And again he pulled himself out on the opposite bank, emerging not a better man, but a different one.

He gave thanks to his white father's god that this time, at least, Singing Bird was not waiting for him. He was finally, blessedly, alone. Gray smoke curled from the chimney in the distance. He had only to climb one more hill, one more mild and thistle-covered hill, and he would be home.

He hid behind the barn when he saw the three men. His little brothers had grown into real Bahannas, with hair on their faces and sun creases around their eyes. He wanted to greet them, to speak with them of Mr. Baldoon and of the days they had shared, but their eyes were red and they were sharing their jug with that other, the one who pointed a gun at him as he watched them from the cliff.

So Walks with Eagles crept on silent Indian feet around the barn and through the bushes, through the milkweed and the sunflowers, tall and dense as an army, to a window where he might be able to look upon the mother who spoke to him with soft coos and warm kisses instead of with shrill caws and hard pecks.

His white mother knelt by a bed, with her back to the window. The bed coverings were disarranged and one of her arms was hidden between the mattresses. She sat back on her heels and pulled out a large feather. Just then another woman opened the door.

India's hair was still yellow as corn, but everything else had changed. On the hill he had wondered if this grown woman could have been his little sister. Now he knew for sure. She dropped to the floor, next to their mother, when she saw the feather. He studied her strong fingers and blunt nails as mother and daughter embraced.

Walks with Eagles stood with the sunflowers, clothed only in a loincloth, and gazed through bleary eyes. One fragile glass window was the world that stood between him and his family.

"Ye canna," Mr. Baldoon whispered in his ear. But when his mother climbed to her feet and turned to go, Walks with Eagles pressed one palm against the pane.

India didn't see him. She rose too, splashed water on her face at the basin, then walked to the window and leaned her forehead against the cool glass. She stood less than five feet from her brother but she never looked up.

"India," he whispered, and was just about to rap on the window and say it out loud when the man with the gun burst into the room.

When the man put his hands on his little sister and lifted her off the floor, Walks with Eagles picked up a rock to break the glass.

"Ye canna," Mr. Baldoon whispered again.

And besides, India was smiling.

"Go now," Mr. Baldoon said, and Walks with Eagles tried to turn but waited just a moment longer to see how she moved and how she spoke but by then it was too late.

When Walks with Eagles finally returned to camp, Little Flower kept her tears of joy and relief and anger locked safe inside. "My husband has returned!" she shouted. "My husband, Walks with Eagles, has this day returned to us! Come see what he carries!"

All the children shouted and came running with sticks to clack. The older ones approached more slowly. Still, even the braves who had whispered about him were impressed by the finery that now adorned the son of their chief, and even the elders who had plotted in a secret powwow what they would do should he return, opened their mouths in praise and genuine reverence when they saw the eagle head on his staff.

Chief Stands and Speaks did not run to his son's side as he would have in earlier days. His heart was filled with sickness and he could no longer summon the strength to rise from the cool earth on which he rested. Carries Much and Touched by the Enemy cared for their dying husband. They fanned him with feathers when he was too warm, and covered him with their own warm bodies when he shivered. They fed him and cleaned him and carried him sometimes into the fresh air when he did not like the smell of himself.

Carries Much was sent by the chief to welcome his son on his behalf. "My son," she said formally, these being the words of the chief himself, "my heart is gladdened to look upon your face once more. There is much to say and much to know. Tonight, we shall all feast in honor of your glorious and safe return. White dogs have been selected and fattened in preparation for this night."

The people cheered at that news and felt their hearts soften toward Walks with Eagles. Carries Much embraced her husband's son and smiled again at Little Flower.

Only Walks with Eagles could not feel the exultation that should accompany a hero's welcome. He let Little Flower lead him into their tipi, let his sons tumble into his lap and gently touch the eagle head on his staff, but he could not let go of the murderous memory that was slicing him in two and carving up his joy: that he had killed one father to please the other.

"You have done it, my husband," said Little Flower as she combed out his hair. "Now your totem is strong and your family is safe." She scooped buffalo fat out of a horn bowl and applied it skillfully to the heads of her sons. They had not yet earned the right to wear their hair long, like their father. "After the feast tonight," she said, "you will be the most respected man of all the Men Among Men." She let her tears flow at last.

"Why do you cry?" Walks with Eagles asked his wife. "Still you are not happy?"

There was a sting to his words that Little Flower had not heard before. She pulled back her tears but did not answer. "They wait for us at the feast," she said, shoving her sons out of the tipi as she spoke. Little Flower was so wounded by the spear in her husband's voice that by the time Touched by the Enemy set the steaming bowl of boiled white dog before her, Little Flower could not even lift up her spoon.

Chief Stands and Speaks rallied his remaining strength for the occasion. With the aid of his wives, he stood by the fire and spoke of the honor that Walks with Eagles had bestowed upon their tribe. Black-Faced Bear might have expressed disapproval, had it not been for the huge meal that lay rumbling in his belly and the troubling silence of his daughter, Little Flower.

Walks with Eagles was required to relate his tale over and over again to the guests in his father's tipi. Over and over, he told of the magical chase over mountains and moons to the Land of the Ghost Trees. Over and over, he described the black forest of scorched trees, and the holes in the earth, and the orange flesh of the fallen pines, and the animals who revered the ground upon which he walked, and the eagle who stood on a stump for him and then bade him shoot.

Walks with Eagles did not describe the voice that spoke to him, nor did he describe his own anguish in obeying what the voice commanded. Nor did he tell them that his first thoughts after the miracle were not for his own people, but for a grieving white woman at a grave site near a river. And for a woman with yellow hair.

He looked at Little Flower after each telling to see if she heard all the parts he had left untold. He had learned, by that time, how to see the pictures and hear the words that live inside the eyes. But Little Flower never looked up at him, so he couldn't know what she heard. I am sorry, my wife, he said to Little Flower with his eyes, but as she never looked up, he couldn't know if she heard that part either.

Chief Stands and Speaks was very pleased. After all of his guests had picked up their bowls and spoons and gone back to their own tipis, he sat down next to his son.

"You have made me very proud," he said. "Now truly can you be called Walks with Eagles." He paused to allow Carries Much to help him recross his legs. "Now am I strengthened with eagle's blood!" he cried, waving his fists in the air, one of them nearly catching Carries Much in the eye. "Now have I found my true son, and the next chief, on the same . . ." His eyes grew dull and his voice faltered.

"Do not worry," said Carries Much. "It is part of his sickness. It has happened before."

Walks with Eagles carried his sleeping father to the doeskin, newly beaten and smoothed for the old man's comfort. He was frightened by the way his father rolled himself into a ball and drooled in his sleep. He looked to Carries Much for reassurance. "What has happened to him?" he asked her.

"You," she said sharply, unexpectedly. "You have happened to him. You have worried and shamed him all of your life." He started to rebuke her but she held up her hand.

"And you have lied to him," she said. "I know all about your 'vision.'"

His eyes flashed. It was not seemly that a future chief should be discussing these things with a woman. But she had always been a kind woman, and good to his father, and he would give her another chance.

"I have redeemed myself . . ." he started to explain, but her eyes flashed too, and before he could finish his sentence he felt her thick hand hard across his mouth.

"Lies," she said. "More lies. I heard from your own thoughts the stories that you did not tell the others." She motioned for him to follow her to the farthest edge of the tipi, where his father would not be disturbed. "And I will warn you," she said, "because you are the love of my love, that you must tell him all of it, and tell Little Flower too. Or your father will die, your wife will turn even your own sons against you, and the woman with the yellow hair will curse your name forever."

He wanted to strike her but could not. No more than he could strike his own mother. He started to leave but she caught his arm.

"Grow up, Boy Found," she said, tears flooding her large eyes. Or you will be lost to all of us, was what she told him with her thoughts.

Walks with Eagles tried to tell them both. He curved his body around Little Flower's that very night and said, "My wife, I have something to tell you." But Little Flower did not awaken and he was bone weary. One night of peace, that's all, he promised himself. I will tell her tomorrow, when she is not so near and warm and soft, and when her hair does not brush against my lips and smell of waterfalls.

Little Flower was already hanging the large kettle over the open fire when he awoke. He watched the movement of her shoulder blades as she stirred the contents with a long-handled spoon. Her neck is so slender, he thought, as she tossed her hair to one side and leaned into her task. He saw the high bones of her spine protrude as she tipped her head to smell the simmering gruel. She is too fragile, he told himself; I must not burden her with more worries. I must protect her from the truth. And each revolution of her heavy spoon only strengthened his resolve to protect, protect, protect, until after a while he grew dizzy with watching the swirling spoon and lost track of what or whom, exactly, he would be protecting.

At length he stood and took the long spoon from her hand. "I will help you," he said gently to his wife. She smiled up at him and sat back on her heels. Tears of gratitude filled her eyes.

This time, instead of being angered by the tears, Walks with Eagles knelt down and kissed them away. Little Flower was ready for him. She returned kiss for kiss, touch for touch, and when she unsheathed for him her long and darting tongue, he became the flute of his ill-fated vision—explored eagerly, mercilessly, every crevice and plane of him—and though he writhed and moaned and wished her never to stop, he finally had to stop her tongue and turn her over and take her in a manly way, lest she have a vision of her own filled, as his had been, with his long ago lives and longings.

"I must go to my father," he told her, after.

"Yes," she said. "He has been very ill." She began at once to tidy up the area, smoothing out the hide, fanning up the fire, even before she slipped her dress back over her head.

He stood at the flap of the tipi and smiled at the tilt of her chin as she hurried about, setting their household to rights again. "You are a good wife," he told Little Flower, though once again he heard the sharp words of Carries Much and the smart slap of her hand on his mouth. He wondered again if he should be telling his wife all of it.

"And you are a good husband," Little Flower responded. She ran to him and replaced the memory of the sharp blow to his mouth with a soft kiss of her own.

I must protect her, he vowed again on the way to his father's tipi.

Chief Stands and Speaks was very pale. He raised himself to his elbows when he heard his son's voice.

"Come," he said. He tried to shout, but the effort made him cough and wheeze. "Come sit beside me," he whispered. He motioned for Carries Much to bring him his pipe. He struck it three times on the ground before offering it to Walks with Eagles. "The healing spirits are all forsaking me," he explained. "I am trying to call them back."

"Good spirits will never forsake you, Father. You are good and brave and will soon be strong again."

The old man shook his head. "Too late. Angry spirits clawed at my throat and then carried bad medicine into my head and my belly. Whenever I eat, it angers them further and they throw the food out of my body."

Walks with Eagles turned on Carries Much. "And you did nothing to help my father?" he said.

Carries Much glared at him then removed herself from the tipi.

Touched by the Enemy dumped a parfleche of dried roots and leaves in the lap of Walks with Eagles. "Mountain ash, black alder, blue cohosh, sassafras," she said, pointing them out and spitting the names in his face. "Wormwood, boneset, blackbush," she continued. "These we brewed into tonics, these we steeped into teas, these we ground and mixed with bear fat into a poultice for your father's chest. And these," she said, pointing to the bark of the juniper and cedar, "we burned into a healing smoke, to cleanse and purify the air." Then she turned quickly and followed the path of Carries Much, leaving Walks With Eagles quite alone with his father.

"My son," said Chief Stands and Speaks. "Why do you insult my wives?" He tapped the pipe again three times on the ground before he brought it to his lips. "Walks with a Limp had already given me up for dead. He said he had conversed with the angry spirits and that they did not want to leave my body." *Tap, tap, tap,* he passed the pipe again to his son. "My women have kept me alive long enough to see you again, my son. This is all I have prayed for."

"My Father," said Walks with Eagles, helping his father lean back on the whitened deerskin pillow and the slender support of reeds and poles his wives had devised for him. "You have fought the Great Bear, and you have killed many enemies." He stood and shook the coup stick before his father's face. "How many coups, Father? Count them yourself!" He was trying to shake the bad medicine out of his father's heart, but it was no use. His father's face and hair grayed before his very eyes.

"I am tired," said the chief, gathering the elk hide closer to his chin.

"But there is still so much I must tell you."

The chief tapped the pipe on the ground again. "Then speak, son," he said, smiling weakly. "For soon you shall be chief and all shall listen to what you say." He sat up suddenly and looked around the tipi in a panic, then pointed at a hapless sparrow that had wandered in at the flap. "Get her out," he shouted, waving his arms in the air. "Get her out!"

Carries Much rushed in and rocked her husband in her strong, soft, cradle arms. When he'd quieted, she whirled to face Walks with Eagles. Her command was cold and hard as hail. "Get her out," she said.

Scherzos

The letter was late. I hadn't seen a letter from my mother in over two months, not since Jesse Jr. was born. Jesse could tell that I was disappointed, I guess, because he left off in his debate with Hank F. Salkeld concerning the virtues of Bull Tongue plug tobacco over that of Stud Horse and came over to put his arm around me.

"It'll get here," he told me, squeezing my shoulders. "Mail's slow, that's all."

Mr. Salkeld gave each of the boys a Tolu taffy. "Mind that you don't swaller it now," he told them as he led me over to the piece goods. "Here's something that might perk you up, Mrs. Walker," he said, whispering so as not to wake the baby. "Just got in a brand new supply. Calicos, ginghams, plaids . . ."

"They're lovely," I said. But I didn't mean it. They were all drab as dirt except for one little scrap of a flower print. "Have you any more of this?" I asked him, just to be polite.

He laughed and shook his head. "I never can tell what women are going to want," he said to Jesse. " 'Fraid that's the long and the short of it," he told me. "But hold on. Ruggles was just leaving as you folks walked in. Maybe I can run catch him."

"Please don't bother," I said, but he was already out the front door. "It's not like I'm going to buy it," I said then, just to Jesse.

Brodie and Cam were busy fingering the fancy display of pistols. The shiny barrels were hanging pointed all in the same direction, in a long row on the west wall beneath the colanders, coffeepots, and kerosene lanterns.

"Don't you boys touch them weapons," I called, irritated that their father made me do the hollering in a public place. Jesse Jr. woke right up and started howling. Jesse Sr. was busy smoothing his palm down the arch of a newly waxed saddle and wouldn't have thought to look up until the boys went ahead and shot each other dead.

I was getting impatient. What did I care about meeting some salesman named Ruggles and telling him pretty lies about his sad little piles of fabric? I jiggled Jesse Jr. to get him to stop his eternal fussing while I drummed my fingers on the black and gold labels of some wooden spools marked J&B Best Six Cord Thread. Why did men move so slow? It's a wonder they ever got anything done. Last time we came into Salkeld's General Store, I found seven grown men just setting around the potbellied stove, whittling poor little sticks into nothing and watching their spit sizzle on the black iron. One of them was telling some ridiculous story about fishing for chickens using hooks baited with corn. I'd had to wait a full fifteen minutes just to get some naphtha soap and a side of salt meat that last time, and it looked like I wouldn't be done any quicker this time around.

But we needed flour and lard and molasses, and we wouldn't make it through the week, much less the month, without at least that much. I also wanted to get a couple of onion sets for planting, and maybe that little wooden flute that Cammie had been pestering me about ever since our last trip to town. And I wanted Mr. Salkeld to buy my eggs from me too, before they got spoiled and it was too late.

The screen door finally squeaked open. "This here's Brewster A. Ruggles," Mr. Salkeld said, holding the man by both shoulders and shoving him toward me like he was a two year old in his Sunday best. "Mr. Ruggles, may I present Mrs. Walker? One of our newest and prettiest customers."

Ruggles removed his hat and bowed low, from the waist. "At your service, madam," he said.

"Pleased to meet you," I replied.

Jesse was suddenly at my elbow. "And I'm Mr. Walker," Jesse said, taking the salesman's right hand in his own and squeezing it. "I'm her husband."

"You have a fine grip there, Mr. Walker," said Mr. Ruggles. "Could I trouble you to help me in unloading a few more bolts of yardage for your lovely wife's perusal? I have them just outside in my wagon."

Jesse looked at me and then back at Mr. Ruggles. "Whatever my wife wants." He threw the words at Mr. Ruggles's face like he was challenging him to a duel.

I smiled and told Jesse that I would like to see the other things, if he didn't mind. I said it mainly to keep the peace, but in truth my eyes were aching to look on something pretty again.

"Very good, madam," Mr. Ruggles said, bowing to me again. "Will you follow me?" he said to Jesse.

"Yessir," Jesse said with a steely smile. He turned to glare at me as he followed the man out.

Mr. Salkeld saw the look that passed between Jesse and me, then jumped up and hurried after the younger men. "I'll help too," he said, running to catch up.

Each man staggered under the weight of three or four (Jesse carried five) bolts of fabric and dropped them on the table before me. This was more like it. The colors were richer, the weights fuller, the textures smoother and softer than any that Salkeld had up for sale.

My fingers flew to a bolt of burgundy moiré. I thought of my mother, of the lemon verbena she always wore, of the long Sundays in church when I'd bury my face in the watery silk of her best gown and fall blissfully asleep until the sermon was over.

"That one comes to you direct from Paris, France," said Mr. Ruggles. "You have excellent taste, Mrs. Walker, if I may say so."

Three town ladies, each with a child in tow, overheard this last remark and rushed over to the table just as I was fingering a royal blue chintz and a lavender satin.

"I'll have ten yards of that, Mr. Salkeld," said one of the ladies, pointing to the chintz. "My curtains are so shabby. The blue will be perfect!"

"I'll take three of the lavender and, oh, I think six yards of that lovely white eyelet for Sarah's frock, don't you think, Mina?"

As for me, I sighed over the silks and an exquisite coral lace, but settled on a sturdy brown corduroy for Jesse and the boys and a soft bone muslin for myself. It wasn't like I'd be going to Paris, France anytime soon.

I was still pawing through McGuffey readers for Brodie and Cam when the three ladies returned with two friends. One of them bought enough yellow calico to outfit all four of her young daughters, and the other, a tall woman with large hands (who kept staring at me when she thought I didn't see her), bought an entire bolt of gray flannel.

When they left, Mr. Salkeld cut off several lengths of the coral lace and set it with my other goods on the counter. "Fair payment," he told me with a wink, "for a job well done."

He nodded toward the new group of ladies who were headed for the piece goods table. "Mr. Ruggles and I have been talking," he told me. "We'd like you to help us, seeing's how he's a bachelor and I'm a widower. We could use a feminine influence around here, to set us straight on what ladies like."

I didn't know quite what they were getting at, but I smiled and said I was happy to help. Jesse was at my elbow again.

"I'd need you to come out when the regular drummers, like Mr. Ruggles here, make their runs to our town. Usually about every four months or so."

"Two," said Mr. Ruggles.

Jesse stepped up to the counter. "My wife has plenty of chores at home," he said. "And three younguns."

"I could take, say, twenty-five percent off the cost of your purchases?" Mr. Salkeld looked at Jesse with his eyebrows raised.

"Thirty," said Mr. Ruggles. "I'll make up the difference."

Jesse spoke to Mr. Salkeld but looked at Mr. Ruggles. "Twenty-five percent sounds mighty fair to me, just for dawdling through some doodads. Thank you." He turned back to the counter. "Could you figure what we owe you now, Mr. Salkeld, and we'll be on our way."

Mr. Salkeld helped Jesse load the sacks of sugar, flour, and the rest of it into our wagon and said that he'd add the total to our bill. "Thank you for coming. . . ."

"And some whiskey," Jesse said. "Put some whiskey in there too. Medicinal."

Mr. Ruggles held the door open while Mr. Salkeld dashed in and back out with the brown bottle, then he took my hand and helped me up into the wagon. "Au revoir," he said as we pulled away.

Jesse sulked for a good half hour on the way home from Salkeld's. "Did you want to do that?" he asked me finally.

"Do what?"

"Work for them that way."

"Looks like I am, want to or not. You got it all arranged for me."

Jesse pulled hard on the reins. "Whoa," he said to the horses. Then he turned on the board to face me. "Just give me the word, gal, and I'll turn these horses right around and tell Hank to forget it. Deal's off."

"Jesse," I said, "he's giving us a twenty-five percent discount just for me to dawdle over doodads. You said it yourself." I haa'd the horses to go, but they never did pay me any mind.

"Hell, I don't care if he gives us one hunderd percent off. I'm asking you do you want to do it." He narrowed his eyes and kept staring at me until I had to laugh.

"Well, don't bite my nose off," I said, trying to frown but still laughing because I did so love to look at that man's sweet face when he gave it to me all at once. "Yes," was my answer. "I do want to do it. I do like to touch velvet now and again."

"Fine, then," he said. "It's all settled." He haa'd the horses back into action and they picked up their hooves so quick you'd think he'd lit a torch on their rumps. "But you watch out for Mr. Brewster Smooth-Talker Ruggles, you hear me? I seen his likes before and I know what he's after."

"Yes, Jesse," I said sweetly, like the accommodating wife he knew I never had been and never would be. Then I slipped my fingers down behind his belt and, "Ah, velvet," I said, and then he started grinning like a jack-o'-lantern. In this manner we took our minds off Mr. Ruggles and the piece goods table for the rest of the ride home.

I'd generally get a note sent home from the school with Brodie on the day before my presence was requested at the store. They were always such lovely notes, filled with phrases like "at your convenience," and "do us the honor of," that it was almost worth my trouble just for the notes alone, even without the 25 percent off part.

But the extra credit sure came in handy, especially after Jesse's deal with the red wheat people fell through. They were supposed to front him for the start-up costs and the seed wheat, and then take a portion of the profits later, after harvest. Except that the "portion" they demanded at the end seemed like it was a whole lot more than they led Jesse to believe it would be in the beginning, and left us with a lot less than we thought we'd have. Fact is, it left us with nothing at all and it was hard on Jesse to have done all that work and have counted on so much and to still have his children wearing old, torn-up brogans to school.

"But at least we've got the equipment now," I reminded him. "And seed wheat of our own. Next year is going to be ours," I said.

"Well, almost," said Jesse.

The "well" of it was that he still owed those people on the tools and equipment, as the profits hadn't been as high as they'd anticipated. But they weren't making us pay on them outright, Jesse explained to me. They were going to let us make payments for another year, with just a little bit of interest—which naturally they had to charge because this was a business arrangement, after all—and after that everything would be fine.

"We've got to be careful about what we sign from now on," I said.

"Yep," said Jesse. And then he poured molasses all over his corn cakes, as he always did, just as if it were already paid for.

So it was a good thing that Mr. Salkeld needed me to help him. The notes started coming home with Brodie more and more. After a while, he put me in charge of choosing the ladies' shoes as well, and after that, picking out the petticoats. After a while, it got to be just like I worked there for real. I'd hitch up the wagon, drop the big boys at school, then take Jesse Jr. with me to the store. Mr. Salkeld kept on raising the percentage of our discount until it got to be over 85 percent off the goods we bought, which worked out to be almost like paying nothing, so that was a very good thing.

And it was fun for me to meet all the drummers. Besides Mr. Ruggles, there were drummers for dry goods and hardware, medicine, grocery, meat, stock feed, chewing gum, firecrackers, you name it. There were drummers for everything, friendly as they could be, and they brought news from other parts, mostly about people I had never even heard of, but sometimes about people who were tied into my own life tight as ribbons in a horse's tail.

The drummers were usually in a hurry, off to the next town and the next. But now and then they'd sit by the stove with the whittlers and the spitters, and they'd bring the world to our little town. They talked about Lincoln and niggers, and they'd fight sometimes about who was to blame for what. And one time the notion drummer, Mr. Francis, spoke about some families he'd known in Oregon. I pressed him for details, as my mother used to tell us of the Gruvers and the Linkes, and sure enough, he knew something about both.

Seems old Mildred Gruver ran shrieking into the mountains one day and no one saw her again. Rumor was that either a bear got her or she was honored in one of the backwoods tribes as a mystical being, a "spider woman," and was greatly reverenced. Course, W. B. took all that pretty hard at first, but after a while he started taking orphaned and hard-put children into his own home, where he gave them hot food and warm beds and taught them to be carpenters. Lem moved to California.

The Linkes' story was even better, and I wrote my mother about it soon as I heard. Seems little Greta and Josiah Linke, Hattie's children, never quite made it to Oregon, leastways not for several years. A hunting party of Shoshone snatched them up one sunny afternoon while they were off gathering firewood for camp. The Indians cared for them, according to all later accounts, and made them their own. They even gave them Indian names. Josiah was called White Shield, for placing his small body between his sister and their drawn arrows. And Greta they called Gray Eyes, because of the long, hard way she gazed at everyone and everything.

Both children grew to love their Indian families, the story goes, and were furious when well-meaning trappers "rescued" them and brought them back to civilization. Greta was eighteen by then, a woman grown, and talk was that she left behind a certain Indian brave to whom she had become seriously attached. Josiah was nearly twenty-one, and already thoroughly wild. As Roy could not be located and was presumed dead, the "children" were returned to the home of Hattie's sister and her husband, who sincerely and enthusiastically attempted to tame them into polite and productive Christians. But every attempt failed miserably, so when they ran off that second time no one tried too hard to bring them back again.

Josiah rode straight back to the Indians and that was that. But Greta was waylaid by a handsome, well-dressed stranger with wavy black hair who promised her the world, apparently, and lured her to his den. Once there, he held a gun to her head, introduced her to his drunk and drooling associates, and explained that she was there to help him pay off his gambling debts to the fine gentlemen present. She did a stint in jail after that, for the cold-blooded murder of a certain Hollingsworth Blankenship, and for an unprovoked assault on a number of upstanding and law-abiding citizens, with intent to do bodily harm. She might have been left there forever if it hadn't been for Hattie's sister, who got wind of the mess and talked sense into the sheriff at his local saloon with the help of her like-minded, stick-wielding ladies from her local chapter of the Women's Christian Temperance Union.

"She kept pretty much to herself after they let her out," Mr. Francis said. "Far as I know." He assured me that he'd tell me if he ever heard anything else about poor Greta, and this I relayed to my mother as well.

It was through the drummers, Mr. Ruggles, in fact, that I heard stories of a lone Indian—a lost soul, according to one of the sillier ladies who passed by just at that point in the story—who'd been sighted at various points throughout the midwest. By most accounts he was harmless enough, never hurt a soul and rarely spoke a word, just sat on his pony with a faraway look in his eyes and an eagle's head skewered on the stick he always carried.

I kept quiet then, though I wanted to jump up and shout I know him, I know him! He's the one who saved my children! And I knew more than that besides, though I never told anyone and I tried not to even think about it. I knew who he was by the way my mother had frozen when she caught sight of him through the tall grass. By the way she'd dropped her hand into her lap. I knew because he'd called me by name and because he'd found my children when I could not. He was my guardian, I knew. My own personal guardian angel. He was the brother who would never have yanked on my pigtails or dropped toads down my dress just to make me scream. He was the good and strong and gentle brother of my dreams, who hovered overhead like a magic eagle and who protected me and my children from danger, from fear, from Singing Bird. His were the invisible eyes that watched over us when Jesse's deep brown ones were bleary with whiskey. And I would never betray my own brother. Never.

Overtures and Finales

Carries Much, Touched by the Enemy, and Little Flower worked together to prepare for the ceremony. They built a scaffold for the body of Chief Stands and Speaks, rubbed sage into his skin, and braided sweet fern into his long white hair. Much food would be needed for the feast. Every squaw in camp was busy grinding corn or mustard seed, or chopping up purslane and scallions, or skinning and stirring joints of antelope into huge kettles over open flames.

Walks with Eagles walked with his children deep into the forest. "My sons," he told them, "after today, your father shall be chief of the Men Among Men."

"Hooray!" shouted the youngest, splashing in the stream.

The eldest son went to his father, now sitting on the bank, and touched his face. "Your words are happy," he said. "But your voice is sad. Why is this?"

A mourning dove cooed in a distant tree. The eldest son searched his father's face for an answer but, finding none, supplied it himself. "It is because you will be leaving us again."

The child turned on the path then and headed back to camp. He would not be comforted.

Carries Much officiated at the ceremonies. She lifted her great arms to the skies. Extravagant flesh cascaded from her elbows; the rippling wonder of it infused her words with a rich and royal significance. She entreated the great spirits to embrace the soul of her dead husband.

"My husband loved the Men Among Men," she shouted to the spirits. "Stands and Speaks was a great warrior who earned many feathers. He never turned to save his own life, and three times faced death to recapture the fallen body of a Man Among Men. Stands and Speaks was a mighty hunter. He killed the Great Bear with a tomahawk alone, and never let our people be hungry. Stands and Speaks was a good husband. He smiled on us often," she said, looking at Touched by the Enemy. "And," she said, turning her gaze to Black-Faced Bear, "never did he strike a woman or a child."

Four strong braves lifted the body of Stands and Speaks and settled it carefully in the high, pine-nestled scaffold. On his chest was placed a single feather, his tomahawk, medicine bundle, and a portion of the ceremonial feast, so that he might be prepared for the long journey over the Ko-go-gaup-o-gun, the sinking serpent bridge, to the land where his ancestors danced and sang with joy. "Please, our chief, go peacefully to the world of the spirits, and intercede on our behalf, that there may yet be an abundance of buffalo and berries, and that we may yet live safe away from the dangers of the Long Knives and the Iron Snakes."

The people held deer tails over the ceremonial fire until the hair was burned away. Then they rubbed the tails over their faces and arms, and over those of their children, to ensure that the dead man's spirit would be discouraged by the offensive smell from entering their bodies and go directly to the Beautiful Land.

Carries Much slashed at her arms and legs in mourning, and the others followed suit, with wails and lamentations. Yellow Fox beat out a rhythm on his drum, and young braves jumped up to dance out the words of Carries Much. They danced about the great deeds and the great kindnesses of Chief Stands and Speaks, and they danced out their own grief with shouts and movements sharp and sweeping.

A red-eyed vireo alighted on the scaffold as they danced, but did not peck at the food on the dead man's chest.

After the mourners had exhausted all forms of lament, Carries Much again stood before the people. She announced that her husband wished for his son, Walks with Eagles, to replace him as chief. The people heard her respectfully and lowered their eyes when Walks with Eagles stepped forward to claim the blood-clotted elk hide that Carries Much had carried with her from Dark River, to Stands and Speaks, and now to him.

Black-Faced Bear stood and sent his thoughts to the red-eyed vireo, who still perched near the head of the dead chief. Look now on your handsome lover, he told her with his eyes. Then gaze upon our esteemed new chief, your pitiable son, a coward and a liar who drapes around his honorable shoulders the blood of a whore.

Chief Walks with Eagles tried to be a good leader. He followed the counsel of Carries Much and walked among his people to ask of their health and needs, to settle disputes between brothers, and to praise the prowess and strength of the hunters who returned with good kills. He was gentle with Little Flower, for he cared for her deeply. She had painted their tipi with pictures of the eagle and the bear and the black forest, depicting her husband's journey and triumphant return with the most powerful of protecting spirits.

But Chief Walks with Eagles was pulled by cruel spirits as well. It wasn't enough that they tugged on his heart, but they pulled at his body too. They pulled so hard that sometimes they opened his eyes in the middle of the night, and pushed him to his pony, and compelled him to ride away. The first few times it happened he'd found Little Flower weeping, and his eldest son angry when he returned. He explained to them that he was not at fault, that it was the spirits that led him away. They looked at him with sideways eyes, but gradually they became accustomed to an empty place by the fire when they awoke. They resolved to weep no more.

In private, away from the eyes of his wife and the others, Carries Much rebuked him for leaving his people. "Your father never left," she told him. And for a long time he accepted these rebukes as just, and asked her forgiveness, and promised to try harder.

But during one of his trips to the other world, Walks with Eagles found his little sister. She was hanging garments on a length of rope and her eyes were swollen and red. Walks with Eagles spoke with his little sister then, and discovered that he could comfort her with his words. She needed him. She might even have needed him more than did the Men Among Men, for they had Carries Much for comfort and counsel. His heart softened when he saw this. And it hardened too.

When he returned from that trip, Carries Much again called him into his father's tipi, and again she tried to warn him of the consequences of his actions. But this time he spoke to her rudely.

"I am Chief Walks with Eagles," he said. "You are only a woman. Do not speak to me this way again."

Because she smiled at his words, he raised his hand and hit her with the back of it, full on the face and hard, so that she fell backward onto the doeskin.

He ignored the lines of blood that trickled from the corner of her mouth, but stood over her, jabbing his finger in her face. "I am Chief Walks with Eagles!" he said again.

"My son," she said sadly, still twisted on the ground. Her eyes said: You are Lost Man now.

If it hadn't been for Jesse acting the way he did, I might never have spoken to him at all. It happened on the day the grasshoppers ate up our third harvest of wheat, along with just about everything else. I'd been tough about it for the first two years, telling Jesse that it wasn't his fault we kept losing money instead of making it, that next year would be better. Or the year after that. But that third time sort of did it for me. I didn't have any more hope left to feed him. I didn't have any more tough left and I just had to cry. Couldn't help myself.

Jesse didn't like it when I cried. He decided that, seeing how he'd already chugged away the last few swallows in his jug, he'd just go off to town and get himself some more instead of sitting there watching me cry into my apron about something he had no hand in.

Except that Mr. Salkeld had had words with him a couple of days before, about the whiskey he kept buying when he should've been worrying about me and another new baby. So he'd have to stay in the saloon, he told me, instead of bringing it home, and that would just about serve me right for not stopping him from drinking so much last week when I should've known that he'd really be needing it now.

I couldn't stop him and I didn't try. I just wandered out back when he left and started scrubbing clothes on the washboard. We had a few things left that the 'hoppers didn't find. A couple of plaid shirts, a few pairs of socks, one suit of overalls. That was about it, except for the clothes on our backs and the linens on our beds. I had hung out the rest of it just before the 'hoppers came. Guess they thought I was laying out their suppers.

I rinsed those last things and pinned them on the line, first pulling off the tiny shreds of lace and flannel that the 'hoppers left behind. Then I looked out on our wheat fields. Russian red wheat. Brought to us lucky folks by the Mennonites themselves. Hardiest wheat ever grown. It would make us our fortune. Indestructible.

All gone.

That was when I sat down next to the pigpen and really let loose. If my crying bothered Jesse before, the way I bawled then would've driven him clear into the next county. I cursed the 'hoppers and the wheat. I cursed the dust and the stupid pigs that rolled in it. I cursed the day I left my mother's big oak hearth and real wood stove, and most of all I cursed Jesse for dropping us here and then skipping away every chance he got to be with his precious whiskey.

I wore myself out with all that cursing and then I felt him. Standing over me. Him and his shadow both.

"India," he said.

I scrambled to my feet and wiped the tears off my face, probably smearing dirt all over it instead.

He smiled at me. "Why do you cry, little sister?"

And of course that did it. Made me cut loose all over again. Last time I saw him up close was when he'd saved my little boys for me, when I'd pretty near given up. So much had happened since then. I pointed to the ruined wheat and blubbered something about my grandmother's lace tablecloth, but I couldn't speak for sobbing and when I hid my face in my hands so he couldn't see how red it was, he put his arms around me and held me until I stopped shuddering and spluttering and could just about breathe again.

I don't know why it seemed so natural to fall apart in front of a mostly pure stranger, but it did. I'd dreamed about my Indian brother for so many years and then suddenly there he was, real and solid and in my own front yard, his buckskin soft and warm against my cheek.

"Do you know who I am?" he asked.

I smiled and nodded and he looked pleased.

"Why did he leave you?" he asked then.

I didn't know what he was talking about at first, but finally figured out that he must mean Jesse. "He didn't leave me," I said. "Had some business in town, that's all."

He took two steps backward and looked me up and down. "You're filled with Iris," he said admiringly. "How is she?"

"Oh, Mama's fine. Just fine," I said. "She started a library in town. Practically started the whole town, come to think of it." I can get real babbly when I'm excited, so I took a deep breath, then grabbed hold of his arm and pulled him toward the soddy. "Come inside," I said, trying to slow down. "I just got another letter. You can read it."

He followed me inside and gazed on my sleeping boys. Jesse Jr. was only just starting to stretch out of his baby fat, but Dwelly was almost brand new and still just the tiniest thing. A halo of soft yellow hair framed his sleeping angel face. My brother touched the feathery ends of it with gentle fingers.

I found the pile of letters and tucked them under my arm, then I motioned to my brother to follow me outside as I juggled a pitcher of cool water and two metal cups.

"I don't want them to wake up until they really have to," I whispered.

We sat on the brick planter Jesse built for me. It once was filled with periwinkles and morning glories, but they died off real quick and now it was dry and barren as everything else. My brother and I read letters aloud and talked about Mama until the sun started slipping into a ravine and streaked the sky with coral.

"I will be here, little sister," he said as he stood to go, "whenever you need me."

I stood up too and held out my hand. "Mama will be so glad to know you're safe."

He didn't seem to hear me. He leaned forward and left a soft half-kiss in my hair before he turned to leave. "Sister," he whispered. "I will guard you with my life."

I guess that half-kiss thing should've made me suspicious even then, but it didn't. Fact is, Brewster Ruggles and some of the other drummers were paying me all sorts of compliments at the store and I was starting to like it. Starting to expect it, even.

Jesse was the one who was making me suspicious. He never saw anything like sapphires in my eyes, or music in the way I walked. Leastways, if he did he sure never let on. I wondered sometimes if he was saving his pretty words for somebody else. I wondered what he did, besides farming, I mean, while me and the babies were up at the store. I wondered why he needed so all-fired much whiskey if he wasn't sharing it with someone else.

Wondering is just about the worst thing a body can do, I decided. That, and needing. Once you start in with either one there is no end to it.

My Indian brother never showed his face at the soddy again. Not until that last time. But after that first meeting I saw him everywhere. Under the elm on my way home from the store. Behind the schoolhouse where I picked up Brodie and Cam. Beside the blacksmith barn when I took the horses to be shod. And once, though I told him not to do that again because it scared the living daylights out of me, he appeared to me like a ghost from up out of a ravine, all sudden out of nowhere. In the beginning I'd always laugh and exclaim at the lucky coincidence. But then it happened so often that after a while even I figured out that it was no coincidence.

"Come home with me," I'd press him at first. "Meet Jesse. I'll make you some supper."

But he never would come home with me, and stiffened when I mentioned Jesse's name.

So we went on as we had been. Meeting at odd places. Pretending to be surprised. I told Jesse about our meetings at first, but Jesse didn't seem to care about much those days, so I started forgetting to tell him.

I was only talking with my brother, after all. It wasn't as if I was doing anything wrong. Just talking. I needed to talk. I needed it like food, I guess, because our talks tasted sweet in my mouth, filled me up, and only just sometimes twisted in my gut to where I felt a little sick, like I was reading somebody else's mail, or sneaking pennies off the church plate.

That's what it felt like when my brother would ask me about Jesse, just like he really wanted to know, and then make his face all flinty when I went ahead and told him about Jesse's smile or the wildflowers he'd surprise me with some mornings in our bed. That's not what my brother wanted to hear, I guess, because he just kept pressing for details about the other—the bad things. And sometimes, God help me, I was feeling so lonely and suspicious and worn out that I told him about that too.

That's the part I would take back if I could. That's what made me hate him later on. That he had crawled inside me like that and made me say things I didn't want to. He'd put his arm around me and he'd talk about trust and confiding and family, and then he'd pull out what he wanted and toss away the rest.

"You don't understand," I said to him often.

He'd smile then and soften his eyes, and sometimes kiss me on the cheek. "I do understand," he'd say. "I'm your brother."

But mostly we'd talk about other things, and I wanted to do that forever. We had so many common memories, and past days were very dear to me. Especially then, when the present days were always so shifty and brittle.

So we went on as we had been. Talking about my mother and about Mr. Baldoon, about our brothers and their silly little wives, about the Big Blue and the fairy forest and the purple phlox that carpeted the meadow in the spring, and "*Je t'aime,*" my Indian brother said to me one day, when evening was just starting to soften the sky.

"Beg pardon?"

"*Je t'aime,*" he said again, looking straight at me. "She used to say that. Do you remember?"

"Yes," I said, digging faster with my twig in the dirt. "Mama used to say that."

I felt him leaning toward me then, his clover breath on my face. I must pull away, I knew that, but his black eyes caught me and all right then, I said to myself. Then this will be the end of it. Good-bye, I said with my eyes but "*je t'aime*" came out of my mouth. And then he held my head between his hands and kissed me. I pulled away once but he dug his fingers into my scalp and kept me there, until I stopped pulling and just leaned into the warm night, the warm mouth, the warm hands suspending me in that warm, black, airless, star-laced place above the dirt brown plains and all right, I said to him with my arms that slowly coiled themselves around his back, with my hands that opened and spread themselves wide to find and touch the absolute finality of the moment, then this is good-bye.

Above us the gurgling cry of the butcher bird stabbed into the brand-new dark.

My brother pressed his palms harder into my temples and held me still like that when he finally took his lips away. His eyes were black stones and his words were black stones too.

"I will never let you go," he said.

I lay awake all that night. I kept tasting the sweet birch and the bitter hops on his lips and every swallow brought him back. I kept smelling the sharp, smoky scent of juniper in his hair, and every breath reminded my hands of all they had learned about the long, deep muscles that corded all the long way down his back and how those muscles leapt at my touch. So I tried not to swallow and I tried not to breathe. And when my blood screamed and kicked inside my veins and simmered in hot springs beneath my skin and sent little earthquake quivers into the fault lines of my flesh, I pressed my arms and legs hard into the mattress and willed myself to keep them rigid like that, stiff as death, until morning.

But then the Life Stone rolled and bounced on my chest. It was carried and crushed by the currents of voices that dove and splashed and leapt, over bays, over Hatties, over angels and boulders, over the same dooming fires that kept licking my groin and burning all the way up to my heart. Get away from him, one of the voices pounded into my ear. But he's your brother, cried another. Too late, said the third.

I really knew nothing about him. Not why he ran away from my parents. Not how he lived, not where. I realized as I lay there, staring at the grassy hole in the ceiling of the soddy, watching the sharp stars gradually fade into pale gray morning, that it was my Indian brother who always asked the questions and I who always gave the answers. And I realized as I lay there, staring at the sleeping man who even then was burrowing his spine into my thigh, the man who carried my shoes and my sons and my most secret sorrows, that I hated my brother for that.

By morning I was bruised and bewildered. I was no closer to answers than I had been the night before. But the long hours in darkness made two things very clear. First, that I must get rid of that damned stone once and for all. And second, that from there on in, I would be the one to ask the questions. And my brother, as I lived and breathed, would sure as hell be giving me some answers or he could just gallop right back to wherever it was he came from.

I waited until Jesse left for the fields, then ran outside and hurled the Life Stone, chain and all, into the sagebrush. Free! I was finally free! My throat felt new and naked; laughter bubbled up from it as from a virgin spring, and a peace, loud as innocence, shut out all the voices.

I heard clumsy steps in the grass and a small voice laughing behind me. Little Jesse. I whirled around and opened my arms to my son, to my life, to everything new and mild and full of morning. He ran to me, laughing. The rattles glinted gold in the early sun. The pointed head was a shaft of silver lightning when it struck my son's brown leg. It happened so fast. He fell before his smile did.

Lost Man wept in the arms of Little Flower. She stroked his hair and whispered, be still, it's nothing. But she was secretly ashamed. And she was secretly afraid. If the Men Among Men were to see her husband debasing himself in such a womanly manner they would lose all respect for their chief, and he would be chief no longer. He felt her shame and fear and pushed the pain into a quieter place. But it did not go away.

The eldest son approached his father. His face was without emotion.

Lost Man searched the boy's eyes for something of the son he had deserted. He found nothing. Neither sympathy nor contempt. "You have been well trained," said the father to his son.

"You will stay with us now," his eldest son said, and it was not a question.

Lost Man gazed upon the faces of his children. "Yes," he said. "I will stay with you now."

He told himself he would stay because it could have been one of them, and not Jesse Jr., who was felled by the snake. One of them could have been taken from him just as easily, and he would not have been there to know. He told himself he would stay because it might have been Little Flower, and not India, who now mourned a son.

But none of that was true. Lost Man opened his arms to his sons. He knew that none of that was true. Only the youngest son stepped forward, and Lost Man caught him quickly in his arms before he changed his mind as well.

The real reason could not be spoken aloud, and Lost Man shuddered when he thought of it. Lost Man would stay with his people because India had sent him away. Because she had looked on him with cold and distant eyes and said that she did not want to see him again.

"Forgive me, Little Flower," Lost Man said. "I should never have left you." And then he buried his face in the hair of his youngest son and wept again.

A vulture circled overhead when they buried Jesse Jr. Get away, I said. I stared at the long, looping ovals she cut into the sky instead of at the gaping rectangular hole that was opening up in front of me. Urging me forward. Tugging at me like a warm, soft bed piled high with pillows. Go on, it said. Lie down and rest.

Jesse pulled me back from the edge and kept his fingers pressed into my waist until it was over.

I shut my eyes but still saw the hole, the blackness, the small body of still another son gone far away without me. Get away, I said to the vulture again, though my eyes were still closed and the preacher was praying. Get away, I said to Lost Man, and I pictured the back of him—long black hair flying out behind, pony's haunches rippling in a gallop—riding away from me. Come back, I said to Lost Man then, and I cursed him for obeying, for reappearing with his eagle staff, if only in my thoughts, especially in my thoughts, at this of all moments, with my husband's good hand still warm on my back and the first shovelful of dirt thudding down on my quiet child and the Life Stone resting once more over my heart, smugly content in its latest victory.

"Get away," I said again, only this time I guess I said it out loud because the people who were walking away from the grave turned around. And Brewster Ruggles ran toward me, I remember, with his eyebrows all twisted with worry. I remember watching his hand reach for my elbow and then hearing the loud blow that cracked near my ear before Brewster fell to the ground. I remember seeing Jesse's eyes small and black and him rubbing his fist. He's not the one who hurt us, I wanted to tell Jesse. But get away get away was all that came out, and I guess I was screaming it then because Dr. Stanton ran over and opened his black bag and someone was pushing my elbows into the dirt and then I felt the prick in my arm. Then the Big Blue swallowed me whole and sucked me down to a place so deep and so cold I could not even kick.

Jesse wanted me to quit working at the store. He said he didn't want me anywhere near Ruggles, and that we could get by without the trifles I brought home from Salkeld's. I wouldn't have minded quitting except that Jesse was dead wrong about Brewster and I told him so, again and again. But besides all that, those "trifles" I brought home, the cornmeal, the red beans, the evaporated milk that I'd started lugging too, since the goat dried up, were all that was keeping our last three sons alive. And Jesse knew it.

So I kept on working at Salkeld's, kept on apologizing to Brewster for Jesse, kept on reassuring Jesse about Brewster, and all the while poisoning myself with the dark secret that might have stopped all of the fighting. It wasn't Brewster or Jesse either. It was something outside of them both. Outside the soddy, outside the store, somewhere, hiding behind the sage, beneath the elm, waiting in the ravine. For me. And it was all my fault. And when it showed itself again—and I always prayed it wouldn't except for the times when I prayed it would—then I'd have to really say good-bye to the magic eagle feather and to the strong, brave, perfect brother I had always imagined would be out there for me when I needed him. I'd have to say good-bye to my last illusions, my remaining innocence, my final, tattered shreds of virginity. I'd borne six babies and been married fifteen years, but I'd never been torn before, not there, not the way he tore me, so deep inside I couldn't heal.

If only he would stay away. Then none of that would ever have to happen. If only my Indian brother would gallop back to the wife and family he took so long in telling me about, if only he would stay deep in the forest, far away from me, then I could begin to sift all of the ugly, the manipulative, the deceitful out of my memories of him. I could catch just the parts of his love that were pure and protective and brotherly, just as he once caught that single eagle feather as it floated softly into his open palm. If only he would stay away, I could forgive him for the rest. In time I could forgive him.

The snow fell softly, relentlessly. Dwelly often hopped into bed with us, but that night even the older boys bundled in. We'd been holed up in the soddy for nearly three days, and I was just starting to feel safe, finally, for the first time since Jesse Jr. died.

It was my own coughing that woke me up that night. I'd caught a chill when the rains came and couldn't seem to shake it. I untangled myself from the web of sleeping males that surrounded me; I decided to find the cough elixir before I woke the whole house.

Wrapped in a blanket from Brodie's bed, I padded around our little soddy in Jesse's red wool socks. It was especially cold and quiet that night. Coyotes too busy shivering to howl, I supposed. And I never would have seen him at all if it hadn't been for the moon. It was full and round, a wheel of bright light, and where it touched the snowflakes it made them glint and glow like billions of little devil eyes.

It made him glow too. Lost Man stood not fifty yards from my window. Just stood there. Glowing. Watching. Waiting. I shivered. It might have been a bear. But it wasn't. It was him, wrapped in hides and wearing snowshoes. His pony was snorting and pawing the snowy ground beside him. "Get away from me," I whispered. But he didn't move. I carried the bottle away from the window and gulped down a burning swallow. There now, I told myself. I will close my eyes and when I open them again he will be gone.

But he wasn't gone. He was still there. And for all I knew he had been coming around for weeks, months, maybe, and I'd just never heard him. But he was there that night. I saw him with my own eyes. He raised his eagle staff to the moon. And then he saw me too.

Interlude

He saw me watching him.

That's why he came. He saw me watching him, and to him that meant something. It meant that it was my fault he came to our soddy. Even though I begged him to stay away. Even though I threatened him. I tried every voice—the kind one, the frightened one, the cold, hard voice that I held over his head like an icicle—but he wouldn't listen. Not to any part of me.

Why? There is the word that will not leave me. I don't understand. If he loved me, then why? And if he didn't, then why? He died for me, because of me. Why?

There is wonder and amazement in my why, but it is not the same why children use to ask about the sky and the grass and the antelope. My why is tainted with the horror of discovery, with the horror of opening my eyes wide on a moonless, starless night, and of not being able to see. Of not knowing whether I am about to step on a rattler, or on buffalo dung. Of not knowing if I should move, run, hide, or just stand still, waiting for it to find me first. Why? When all I did was care for him? When all I did was try to help?

Well, maybe that wasn't all. But those were my first impulses. My strongest. My best. And for a long time they were my only.

Stay with me. Those overtures were so close to those finales. And here comes the part I did not want to see again.

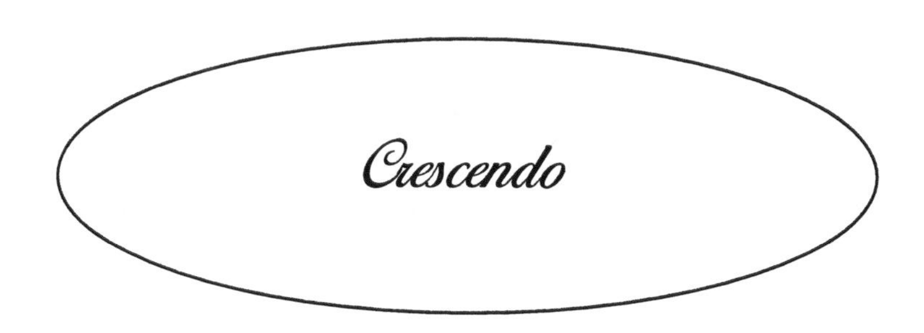

Crescendo

Here's the scene: July 15. Dwelly's third birthday. The sunlight bounces off the white-hot earth to leap and quiver along the parched plains.

I am inside the soddy, wiping my face with my apron as I mix up the batter and stoke up the oven to bake some of Mr. Baldoon's famous Dundee cakes. Jesse has not spoken to me in weeks, not since I told him about my Indian brother, and what I'd done, and where he'd touched me, and how his words had finally frightened me. And how, when I told him again to go away, his fingertips had pressed into my throat.

Jesse stayed with me, but he was different after that. Brittle and buckled as the cracked plains. He went off by himself a lot, and sometimes I'd hear him dry heaving in the outhouse, like he was trying to cry but didn't know how.

But he stayed with me. Even after all that. And now I am trying, in spite of everything, to bake some joy and normalcy back into our crumbling family. Jesse is out back doing God knows what, hoeing the dirt or inspecting our withering bean vines, or maybe just kicking the rocks around with the pointed toes of his boots, I don't know—anything to stay away from me.

The big boys are at school, and little Dwelly is amusing himself out front by the chopping block, scaring up lizards. I told Dwelly that if he'd leave me in peace that morning there might be a little party just for him that afternoon.

I am just breaking an egg into the batter when I feel him. Dwelly is still chattering out front, pleading with a lizard. But something is wrong.

"Dwelly," I call, "come in here this minute." I drop the egg in the bowl and wipe my sticky hands on my apron as I hurry out front. I am crazy. No one there.

"Come give Mama a love," I say, kneeling and holding out my arms to my youngest. His hair is sun yellow, soft and hot on my cheek, smelling of dust and sunshine. If angels can walk the earth then one is living in my Dwelly. His plump arms around my neck are a church with real stained glass windows; he is always flooded with light, and I could kneel there with him forever, encircled by his perfect love.

I close my eyes—that is my mistake—to savor my angel so blindly that I cannot see the demons that hide in every shadow. Dwelly is ripped from my arms. I jump to my feet but see no one. I scream for Jesse but he is already there, struggling behind a cloud of dust with some invisible opponent.

Dwelly. My arms still warm with his buttery touch. Where is he? The wind gusts suddenly from the east and blows the parched and useless land into stinging, blinding swirls around us. I see a flash of yellow hair and a glint of metal by the chopping block. Dwelly. I run into the whirlwind of sand and wind and lethal fists and swinging hatchets, but see only ravens, ravens everywhere, pecking at my face, my arms, my eyes. "God damn you," I shout at Singing Bird. I swing at the birds with my fists, try to gouge them with my nails. No use. My hands and face are pecked bloody but still I hear the sickening thud, thud of fist against flesh, man against man. Love against love. It is a fight to the death now, but I am no longer the prize. Now it is a battle between salvation and destruction: Jesse fighting to save all of us, Lost Man fighting to destroy every last unbearable hope for that.

And it is my fault.

Dwelly screams and calls for me. Too much. I may not have been a good woman but neither was I evil enough to deserve all this. I beat back the ravens and fly into the soddy for a gun.

"Stop," a voice says when I come out again. The voice comes from my throat but it is not my voice.

For one still, miraculous moment, everything stops. The ravens disperse, the wind falls away, and I see it all clearly: Dwelly's yellow hair in

Lost Man's left fist, a hatchet in Lost Man's right, Jesse reaching for his son, Dwelly grabbing at the air for me. They stare at me and the shotgun, all three of them, as if suspended in time, as if needing to tell me something—something that will change everything forever—but unable to speak.

Dwelly breaks the spell. "Mama," he cries, and at that moment the hatchet comes crashing down on the block and my shotgun explodes. I run through the smoke to my baby but the chopping block is suddenly miles away and I run and run but cannot get there. When I finally reach it I find Dwelly sitting on the block, still as ice, gazing dully ahead with dry and frozen eyes.

Lost Man's body lies on the ground beside him; the blast from the shotgun blew a hole clear through his heart.

Jesse is on the ground too, but I fall to my knees and can still, thank the heavens, hear him breathing. A pool of dark liquid is puddling around his right wrist.

It is then that I notice the severed hand that rests quietly on the block beside my silent son.

I remember carrying Dwelly back into the soddy. I remember that his arms and legs wound themselves around my neck and waist and wouldn't let go. I remember that he only loosened his grip when I explained how I needed to go bring his papa inside too. I piled coverlets and pelts on his tiny shivering body, then hurried out to reclaim my husband.

I have never fainted that I know of. Even when I have wanted to, even when it would have been the smartest thing to do, I have never permitted myself that kind of escape. But I can think of no other way to explain away the holes in my memory.

I remember getting behind Jesse and hooking my hands under his shoulders. I pull and pull, and the puddle of blood at his wrist leaves a little river in the dirt. He is so heavy; it's like he's been staked to the ground. I remember trying hard not to look at the hole in Lost Man's chest, or the white hard hand that still rested on the block. If I looked at those things I would freeze solid and never move again. I remember thinking that. "Oh, Jesse," I cry, "I'm so sorry," and I kiss his lips, now burning in the blistering sun, and I know that I need to get him inside, and stop the bleeding, and make everything all right again.

But I don't know how to do any of those things. I want my mother. I sit down in the dirt and the sun and I rock Jesse in my arms and I cry for my mama, just like I was a baby myself, cry for my mama to help us, to help me, and then the last thing I remember is looking up and seeing three women standing over me. The brightest one bends down and kisses the top of my head. She smells of lemon verbena and tells me not to be afraid. The woman in gray is busy taking in all the sights—I am only one of many. The third one studies me, but I have to close my eyes. She looks too much like Singing Bird.

Next thing I know, I am in my own bed with Jesse. Maybe it was all a dream. I want it to have been a dream. Jesse is still asleep, but his face has been washed and his wrist is wrapped up in clean white bandages. They stopped the bleeding, whoever they were, and I wish I could have seen how they'd done that. Dwelly is not in his bed, but for some reason I am not worried. I am not afraid either. I am not anything.

I wander outside. The chopping block has been freshly scrubbed. I check the scene coolly, as if taking stock of Mr. Salkeld's supplies of fishhooks and thimbles. I am not even surprised to find that both the severed hand and Lost Man's body have been removed.

Brodie and Cam are just getting back from school. Their satchels are slung over their shoulders. Their heads are craned to the skies. It looks to all the world as if no one has ever been murdered, or mutilated, or betrayed.

I wave to my sons and get back to my Dundee cakes. My hands are not my own. They are shaking and more shriveled than I remember. But they still know how to tilt the bowl, how to cream the butter with the back of the spoon, how to scrape the batter off the sides as they work. Making Dundee cakes seems the only thing left for my hands to do. But they are doing it so slowly. They wait for the whole world to revolve before they finish dragging that spoon around that bowl.

Brodie and Cam take forever getting themselves into the soddy. I want them with me to surprise Dwelly at his party.

I tiptoe outside so Jesse can sleep. "Shake a leg," I say. I touch my mouth to make sure it is smiling. "What are you looking at anyway?"

"We saw this bird," Brodie says, still looking up. "But then we lost it."

"It was real yellow," says Cammie. "Like the sun."

I stopped smiling then. So that's how it works. The payback. Just like everything else. I wiped the hands that were no part of me on an apron that I'd never seen before, then ducked back into the soddy.

When the cakes cooled I brought them outside and offered them up to the heavens, for any yellow birds who might be passing by. "Please," I said aloud, and repeated the word all night in my bed. Please let it have been the bright one who taught my Dwelly how to fly.

Carries Much summoned Little Flower to her tipi. Touched by the Enemy brought her the message and would stay to watch over her sleeping sons. The light had not yet broken the darkness when Little Flower threw her blanket over her shoulders and ran from one tipi to the other. She was frightened.

"My daughter," said Carries Much when Little Flower arrived. She stroked her hair and bade her sit before she spoke again. "Your husband is here," she said finally.

Little Flower's hand flew to her throat, but she did not speak. Her eyes narrowed as she searched the tipi for the man who had abandoned and disgraced her. She had lain alone many nights in the darkness, dry-eyed and shivering, filling the cold, empty space beside her with buffalo robes and hate, planning the words for this moment. Her sons had given up asking for their father. She would not allow womanly tears to cloak her anger or to choke her words.

"Then let him show himself," she said. "So that I may spit on his face."

Carries Much shook her head and put a large soft arm around Little Flower. "My daughter," she said again. "He cannot." Then she bent to lift the elk robe that covered Lost Man, just enough to reveal his ashen face.

Little Flower did not move.

"I found him just outside my tipi," Carries Much explained. "About an hour ago, when I rose to say my prayers." She shook her head again.

When Little Flower reached for the elk robe, Carries Much caught her hands. "Don't," she said gently.

But she couldn't stop her, Carries Much knew, any more than Little Flower could stop herself from peeling back the hide and exposing the hole in Lost Man's heart.

"Liar," Little Flower whispered when she saw it. But when she slipped her own small fist into the hole and then gazed at the bracelet of dried blood on her wrist, when she growled then shouted, "Liar!" and pounded on his chest, "Liar!" she kept shouting, then Carries Much called to Touched by the Enemy and the two of them wrestled Little Flower away from the body of the fallen chief and back into the tipi of her own frightened and fatherless sons.

The ceremony was a short one. There was no feast. No dancing. Carries Much presided, as she had over every tribal function since the disappearance of Chief Walks with Eagles. A mourning dove cooed throughout, but Little Flower never wept. The Men Among Men listened restlessly, shifting from foot to foot, and shot glances at the darkening sky. A storm was approaching.

Lightning followed hard on the first explosion of thunder. It struck a nearby juniper just as the strongest braves were bearing Lost Man's body up onto the branches of the ceremonial pine. One of the braves was startled into dropping his burden and Lost Man's head nearly touched the earth. Carries Much clapped her hands and the braves scrambled to retrieve their charge.

It was a dry and painful storm. Much flash and great noise, but no release. The sky has forgotten how to cry, Little Flower told her sons.

The juniper was burning. Carries Much touched the shoulder of Yellow Fox, indicating that he and the other young braves should run and fetch water from the river.

Black-Faced Bear stood and blocked their way. "Let it burn," he said, interrupting Carries Much in her final words over the body of the dead chief. "Let him burn too," he said.

The Men Among Men fell silent. Thunder rumbled like war drums and lightning fired up the sky. Carries Much held up her broad hand and fastened her gaze on Black-Faced Bear. The children ran to their mothers, and even the elders moved aside to let her pass. Touched by the Enemy tried to catch her friend's arm, but Carries Much shook her off and did not stop.

Carries Much positioned herself between Black-Faced Bear and the group of young braves. "Get the water," she said to Yellow Fox, and when they'd gone she turned to face Black-Faced Bear. His breath was hot and foul. She wanted to shut her eyes again, as she had in the forest so many years before. But she did not. "So," she said, biting off each word with her teeth. "You would dishonor even the dead."

Black-Faced Bear felt all the burning eyes of the Men Among Men. They could see him under his garments. They could see the softness of his flesh. They could see his limp and withered manhood dangling between his thighs. They did not make a sound, but he knew that they were laughing at him.

"Shut up," he hissed at Carries Much, with his jowls clenched and his fingers round the handle of the war club he now kept always on his wrist. He told her with his eyes that he would kill her if she didn't. That he should have killed her long ago, that he should have beat her harder, harder when he'd had the chance, while her skirt was up and her arms pinned down, that he should have beat her bare flesh until it fell off her bones, until no one, not Dark River, not Chief One on the Wind, certainly not Runs Swiftly, could have found her or known her if they had, until no one could have heard her words, no one could have blamed him, condemned him to this life of humiliation. Of bowing to adulterers, to bastards. To her.

Carries Much heard his silent words. She remembered the crash of his fist on her jaw, the sharp rocks digging into her back when he mounted her, the blows to her buttocks, her thighs, his snarled words, his moans hot and hateful in her ear.

"I will not be quiet," she said aloud. "There is much that our people should hear."

His jowls twitched convulsively and his blood darkened beneath his skin. Then he smiled and kept his thoughts quiet. He loosened his grip on the club and lifted his hand to her face. While all the people watched, Black-Faced Bear traced the outlines of her eyes, her mouth. He stroked her thick hair and let his fingers run down the deep crease of her spine. The mourning dove cooed loudly from the scaffolding and flapped her dusty wings. When Carries Much tried to pull away he wrapped both arms around her. Then Black-Faced Bear buried his face in the many folds of her neck and "Oh, my love," he moaned, "my fawn-eyed love."

With a snap of her head it was over. Carries Much lay crumpled at his feet. Touched by the Enemy cried out, but no one else moved. No one else made a sound.

Black-Faced Bear tried to shove her body aside with his foot, but could not. So he stepped over it and then strode with slow, stately steps to the base of the pine. He stood where Carries Much had stood just moments before. The Men Among Men struggled to understand, to reconcile the discordant images—their powerful queen lying lifeless on the ground, this impotent monster standing upright in her place.

The mourning dove shrieked down from the scaffold that supported Lost Man and stretched out her claws. "I am chief now," Black-Faced Bear was declaring as the bird landed on his face. She dragged her claws across his cheeks before he ripped her off and hurled her into the smoldering juniper.

"Now!" Black-Faced Bear shouted, taking a step forward and holding high his silver-studded weapon, "I am Chief of the Men Among Men!" Black blood dripped from the wounds on his face. "Now you shall do as I say!"

"You," he said, seizing a thin, young brave named Little Horse by the hair and pushing him toward the ceremonial pine, "you shall knock down that bastard's corpse and leave him for the vultures." When Little Horse did not move to obey, Black-Faced Bear swung his huge black paw and knocked the young brave to the ground.

"Move!" he commanded, but Little Horse did not. When Black-Faced Bear whirled to face his people his jowls were jerking again. "You see?" he said to them, pointing at Little Horse as they closed in around him. "He did not obey me." His eyes were wild but he kept talking. "I am chief," he kept saying. "It's my turn." He looked around for Carries Much. Carries Much could always calm her people. Her people loved her. It wasn't fair. "Help me," he whispered when he caught a glimpse through the crowd of her crumpled doeskin dress in the dirt.

Little Flower threw the first stone.

Decrescendo

After Lost Man was found and Jesse mangled, I stopped working at the store. Jesse didn't ask me to that time. I just did. I didn't want to hear any more of the drummers' stories. I didn't want to finger another yard of eyelet, pour another sticky quart of molasses, stack another cast-iron skillet. I didn't want to do anything, see anything, help anyone. Only Jesse. I wanted to help Jesse. I wanted to stay beside him, and fetch him things, and cook his food, and most of all I wanted to keep my face before him, even if he would not look at it. I wanted him to know that I was still there, that I never had and never would leave him. I hoped that my wife face, my morning, noon, and night face, trying to comfort, trying to please, trying to redeem itself, might gradually erase the face he saw—the face that had smiled for another man, and brushed the lips of another man, and betrayed his secrets to another man.

So every morning, I would fry up some hoecakes, let my last two sons wriggle out of my desperate hold to go off to school, look up into the vast blue sky just in case something yellow might be there looking back at me, bid good-bye to my husband as he stared silently at the door, and then set off for the fields, to do the work that Jesse couldn't.

I never was a frail or puny woman, never fragile like my mother, but plowing the fields was harder than it looked. I was hoping to tear up my grief as I tore up the earth, but though I pushed and grunted and swore like a cowboy, for a long time nothing moved.

It was hate that got me going. I tried all the rest of it first. I reached backward for strength, past all the guilt and shame, back to Mr. Baldoon, back to my mother in the corn fields, back to my coffee brown Jesse at the well. But all of that weakened me, made more cracks in a dam that was already bursting, and I sprung first leaks, then springs, then torrents of tears without end, without relief, without comfort or purpose.

So I had to try something else. I had to reach in a different direction for strength. I found my direction at Dwelly's funeral, when our friends from town planted teary kisses on Jesse's cheeks, clasped my last two sons to their sympathetic bosoms, and turned their backs on me.

All except Stewey. He put his arm around my shoulders and let me fall on him when he told me the news that splintered my already broken heart into a million icy chips. All the rest of them turned their backs on me.

That was when I found my way. I reached back into my memories of Boy Found—his brother-words, his lover-touch, his fist in my Dwelly's yellow hair—and what I pulled from his entrails then was a solid rock of hate. I touched the stone that dragged on my neck and realized I had been wearing that rock all along, and when I returned to the fields the next day I moved that plow and I split the earth. I lit into work same way Jesse had lit into Lost Man, back when he still had two hands.

And all the while that vulture, Singing Bird, was circling overhead.

I didn't have many reasons to live in those days. Lining up corners—folding tablecloths and dishrags—that was one of them. Placing edge to edge and smoothing out the crease. Matching socks, toe to toe, heel to heel, stacking them so all the tops were facing upward, as they should be, ready to be lifted with one hand from the drawer and drawn like casing, with one hand, around my husband's foot.

I lived then for the smell of turned-over dirt, the splash of cool water on my face, the sharp elbows and dirty knees of the only two males left on earth who would still touch me. Only that pulled me up every morning and pushed me into my clothes. That, and my unspeakable hope, thin as greased paper, that maybe one fine day Jesse might sneak up behind me again while I was busy snapping beans or rolling biscuits and poke at my ribs with his thick fingers and pull me down with him laughing into his lap.

My mother's funeral followed hard on Dwelly's. That was the news Stewey brought me. That was why he put his arms around me and let me fall on him. My mother had died. Drowned. She'd jumped up and told Stewey that she heard me calling. Then she got jittery as a colt, he said, and couldn't sit still. She drowned crossing the Republican in a boat named *Fortune*. It happened, he said, on July 15.

I'd barely shook the creases out of my black dress before I had to fold it into the trunk for the trip back home.

Jesse surprised me with his offer to go along. "I'm still your husband," was all he said, but he dusted off his shiny black church boots with his one good hand and fit them into the corner of the trunk beside the boys' best Sunday britches.

"She always wanted to be laid out next to Angus and Hattie," Stewey told me. "So I done that already, but I know we'd all feel better if there was a service just the same." He paused to grind the heels of his hands into his eye sockets. "But you don't need to worry none," he said. "They found her real quick, still floatin' in the river. A good farmer and his wife brought her all the way home," he said, "personal."

Singing Bird had to go. After everything she'd shared with the good Bahanna, given to her, taken from her, she had to go. She changed herself into the mockingbird, that being the form her friend had loved best, and sang in an aspen while scores of Bahannas, hundreds perhaps, wept and fell silent and wept again at the words of the man with the cross on his chest.

Only India did not weep. She trembled instead, like the leaves on the aspen. She threw the first flower on the grave mound, then clutched at the stone at her breast and walked quickly away.

Singing Bird winked at a woman in a gray dress, then called to her friend in her sweetest voice. "It's time, Iris," she sang. "Come with us again."

She smiled when she saw how easily Iris could understand her words.

No language came between them anymore. A circle of bright light floated up from the mound of earth, growing larger and brighter as it rose. It danced over to Brodie and Cam and bounced about their heads until they lifted their eyes again and cuffed at each other like bear cubs.

Then it flew to Jesse, brighter than ever, and rested on his right shoulder. It stayed there for a long time. The light wavered and paled before it surged once more, finally lifting off, light as a butterfly. Jesse tugged at his knotted sleeve, then strode away from the gravesite. He would find his wife.

India had taken herself behind a grove of trees. Her mother used to take her there, among the ferns, to look for fairies. They'd never found any. They're all hiding, her mother had told her. But India wanted to find them now. Three good fairies, like before. She needed to find them. She lay down in the ferns and the grasses, willing herself to faint, to die, thinking that that might make them save her again.

Singing Bird flew behind Jesse, following him. She settled on a nearby birch to watch.

Jesse saw India's black dress before he saw her yellow hair. He found her curled up tight in the grasses; she looked like a black stone tossed carelessly into a river of green. If he didn't hurry she would be swallowed up and carried away.

He called her name but she didn't look up. Just climbed to her feet and brushed off her skirt. She started when he touched her hand, but would not let him see her face. Jesse's right arm hung limply at his side, the shirtsleeve knotted at his wrist.

"Iris," Singing Bird called. Both Jesse and India turned to look at the mockingbird. Just then the bright light puffed itself into a huge iridescent flame and charged through both their bodies at once. "Mama," India said, weeping suddenly. Jesse touched her hair with his good hand. Then he lifted his knotted sleeve and drew her close.

There had been too many *I*s already.

"Time to move forward," I told Jesse when our daughter was born. We needed to decide on a name.

"How's about *J*, then," he said, leaning back in his chair. He was chewing on a piece of straw and smiling on me with his whole face.

"Suits me," I said. "We wouldn't want to move too far forward all at once."

He narrowed his eyes and waved his straw in my face but he was still smiling, bigger than ever. He liked it when I sassed him. I opened my blouse to nurse our new daughter because he liked it when I did that too and I would do anything to keep that man smiling. It was my air, his smile, and I'd been gasping for it for so long.

"What do you think of Jemimah?" I asked.

He spit the straw onto the floor.

"Josephine? Jocelyn? Judith?"

He took the baby from my arms and cradled her in his own. "Did you hear that?" he whispered to the baby. He held her face close to his own and lifted his eyebrows high, like he was shocked by my suggestions.

"Pardon me, but I'm not hearing any brilliant ideas coming out of your papa's mouth," I told the baby.

Jesse laughed and shook his head. "Hoooey," he said to the baby. "Your mama's full of vinegar today." He tickled her tiny nose with his own. "I'm surprised that milk ain't gone all sour."

"Well, what do you like?" I asked, standing up and wrapping my arms around the two of them together. I whispered "cowboy" in Jesse's ear to make him shiver.

"You gonna get it, woman," he said, smiling. Then he told me that there was only one name in the world pretty enough for that pretty little babe. "Jessamine," he said.

I watched as he lay our daughter gently on the bed, close up to the wall where she couldn't fall off. He covered her with the afghan I'd retrieved from my mother's house after she died. She was his, all right. Only fitting that he should be able to lay claim to something after all he'd been through. Now that we were finally safe.

"Suits me," I said. But I did want to steer clear of any more *I*s. Not to mention eyes. I was getting real superstitious, I guess. "How 'bout we spell it with a *y*?"

"A why?" he asked. "Oh, I get it," he said then. "Makes no never mind to me how we spell it," he said. "So long as she's still mine."

Then he reached up and poked the thick fingers of his good hand into my ribs and then he pulled me down, laughing, into his lap.

We had seven good years after that. Jesse stopped drinking and the wheat started paying. We added another side to the soddy and planted new wildflowers on the roof. Brodie and Cam were growing through their clothes faster than I could stitch them together. Both took themselves jobs in town—Brodie with the blacksmith and Cammie as the piano player at the Lucky Hands Saloon. He's too young, I told Jesse, when Cammie brought us the news. Jesse agreed with me too, but as the boys still helped out with the plowing and the planting and the harvesting, there wasn't really too much to object to. And the money was something. Money for sugar and real coffee. For a new cedar bucket, a horse collar, and a big hoop of yellow cheese. For a porcelain pitcher and respectability. The money bought us respectability too.

I started to go into town again. Into Salkeld's store, and into the new millinery that started up. Some of the folks nodded at me again, then they smiled, and then they even spoke. Brewster Ruggles still wouldn't look me in the eyes, but he took both my hands in his when he saw me and held them for a while. "We missed you," he said, staring at a bolt of the most god-awful polka-dotted broadcloth I ever did see.

I missed them too. I missed being part of a world that kept checking its watch fobs and listening for train whistles. "I'll be back," I told Mr. Salkeld, "just as soon as Jessamyn gets a little more grown."

But I never did go back. A cough I'd been fighting for years just sort of settled in my chest then and wouldn't go away. I kept it from Jesse for as long as I could, but I knew what was coming even if I never did say it out loud.

Course Jesse knew anyways. I could tell by the way he started rising at the crack of day to light the stove before my feet could feel the chill from the packed-dirt floor. I could tell by the way he'd rush to take the water bucket out of my hands before I sloshed it on my clothes. By the way he stopped telling me things. He told Brodie and Cam what he'd heard about a deserted Indian village, about a body they'd found in a fire pit with its head bashed in and its wrist and ankle tendons slashed. His own people, he told the boys, had done that to him, then held him down with long sticks to die in the flames. They found his war club still clenched in his hand.

"Why didn't you tell me?" I asked Jesse, after overhearing the boys.

"Didn't want to upset you," he said. Which made me really wonder, since used to be Jesse liked nothing better than to tell me about Indians who got theirs, and the grislier the method, the better. "And besides," he said. "It happened a long time ago."

I knew Jesse knew. Because he didn't even argue when I mentioned that I'd really like to go back home for a while. To show Jessamyn where I'd grown up. To show her the fairy forest and the ranging cabin. To let her swim with me in the Big Blue.

He knew what I meant. That I wanted to fill her with enough family stories now to keep her from starving later. I wanted her to drink from the well where Jesse and I fell in love, to wander through the same grasses that once swallowed up her big brothers, to climb the tree where the mockingbird lived, to charge through the wild purple phlox as Iris had when W. B. ran out to greet them. I wanted her to inhale for herself the stories that still hung in the air. Of the Gruvers, of Stewey and the boarding-house men, of Mr. Baldoon and Iris in the kitchen, of Boy Found in the corn fields. Of Singing Bird.

There was so much still to teach her. She would need to know how to darn a sock, make cock-a-leekie soup, boil up ash and lard for soap. She would need to know how bodies worked, how hearts worked. How sometimes nothing worked but how you go on anyway. I wanted to take long walks with my daughter, to show her the colors that were everywhere growing beneath our feet, brushing up against our legs, flying over our heads.

I needed to show her the flowers that grew right out of solid rock.

Jesse knew what I meant. That I wanted to be laid to rest beside the Big Blue, right close to my mother and father, and Hattie Linke.

He made the travel arrangements with an efficiency I never saw in him before. Brodie and Cam were to stay with the farm so Jesse could come with us. I never really said good-bye to my sons. I couldn't figure out how. Cammie said I felt bony when I gave him a squeeze, and Brodie shot him a threatening look. We all had to be careful after that, so we just smiled and I kissed their sweet faces and none of us spoke again.

Lucille and Ruby Nell weren't as bad as I'd remembered. They'd both calmed down a great deal, in fact. Turned into passable good cooks, dressed our beds in clean linen, fussed over Jessamyn, and didn't ask too many questions. Hugh and Henry had done all right.

"Je t'aime," I said to Jessamyn each night as I settled her into my old

bed, the one that used to hide the eagle feather between its goose-down mattresses. We took long walks together, my daughter and me. We picked berries and ate handfuls as we walked, letting the juices run down our chins, pocketing the extras for pie later on. We saw lizards, skunks, raccoons, and one time an opossum with eight babies on her back. We stooped to study heartsease, columbine, sweet verbena, pussytoes, shooting stars, and little green bugs that shimmered in the sun like emeralds. And when I showed her some wild roses that grew straight out of a rock, Jessamyn plopped herself right down in front of them and wasn't satisfied until she'd gotten herself pricked by their skinny thorns.

But we didn't actually talk as much as I thought we would. I wanted to tell her about life—what to do, how to act, how to be. I wanted to tell her quick, so she would know. But I couldn't. I didn't know how. Experience didn't count like I thought it would. Not when it came right down to searching for the words that could keep her safe.

So we talked about the way killdeer birds protected their babies, the way mourning doves in flight sounded like wheat being winnowed, and the way my mama used to make us wash our bare feet in a basin by the door before she'd let us in the cabin. We sang loudly in the woods to make ourselves heard above the roar of the river. We sang Christmas songs, and then we sang about sixpence and blackbirds and pies. And in the end that was fine. It was enough.

And then there was only one thing left for me to do.

"Je t'aime," I said to Jessamyn that night as I tucked the periwinkle blue comforter up under her chin.

I wrapped up in Jesse's overcoat and walked far out into the darkness. The aspens glowed white in the moonlight. The Big Blue roared steadily into the night, rushing past my still self, gouging out chunks of earth in its way. A mockingbird sang in a red cedar. I thought I smelled lemon verbena.

I lifted the chain over my head and held the Life Stone in my palm. It was pale gray—the color that I'd always imagined gentlemen's lapels might be. I wished all of a sudden that I could have known my grandparents. I would have liked to have met my rich grandfather and his beautiful French wife. To have seen my mother and her sisters as they fanned themselves beneath the live oaks and the hanging moss at their plantation.

My arm was not very strong. The weight of the Life Stone alone was almost more than it could bear. I thought about burying the stone somewhere, deep in the dirt where no one could find it. But I threw it instead. Threw it with the last of my strength far away, far, far away from my sleeping angel, my grieving husband, my failing lungs. I had hoped the gray stone would arc and fly in the black sky like a shooting star. But then the coughing started again. And then the blood. I never saw where it landed.

The last thing I remember is Jesse's knotted sleeve pushing back my hair.

Coda

Look.

A pastel gauze is floating down around me now. It is soft as rabbit pelts, warm as flannel, cool and smooth as watered silk. It is softening the white light so that I can finally look into it. It is sifting all the ache into something like compassion. It is filtering my past into something I can bear, sometimes savor, almost understand.

And my daughter will find the Life Stone of Singing Bird. Even though I've done everything I could think of since the day she was born to keep that from happening.

But I am glad. That's the strange part. I am glad that she will find it because it is filled with Iris and me too. As much as it is with Singing Bird. There, I said it. I am glad. Glad to the brink of fear.

Greta will help her. I am glad of this too. Greta was there with my mother. Trapped with her in Purgatory Pass, tied to her in the Big Blue. Hers were the round, resolute eyes that peered from the circle of the Conestoga canopy. Greta was the one, I see now, who bought me a job at Salkeld's store with her bolt of gray flannel. And later, when I sat in the dirt and the blood, my fingers hooked beneath my husband's shoulders, she was the one in gray, an angel in a mortal frame, observing me in all my grief and madness.

So it is fitting, I think, that Greta be the one to save my daughter. She is the link between Iris and me, Jessamyn and Singing Bird, Angel and

Artist, all of us together tangled like loose threads into knots tight as symphonies.

And it is fitting, I see now, that Boy Found was the one who saved her. Remember that part? Boy Found rescued the Shoshone brave and his gray-eyed squaw. That was Greta too. It was a small part but an important one, as it turns out. It changes everything, in fact. It changes Boy Found and Lost Man. It changes me.

I am different now. I can begin again.

We can all begin again. Listen.

It made no difference, finally, whether Singing Bird was invisible or not. No one saw her. The dark procession of bending figures trickled past like rolling tears. Six of them shouldered a great wooden box.

A girl child with yellow hair trailed behind the great box. From time to time she'd reach up and press a tender palm against a sharp corner, then stop to examine the round mark left in her flesh. She made soft sounds like raindrops falling on a lake. The sounds fell into a rhythm with her footsteps. Singing Bird glided through the shadows to follow, her coral bracelets tinkling faintly as she moved.

Jesse didn't know. He never had seen Singing Bird. Never had even quite believed she existed, despite the tales his wife told him, despite the rock his wife always wore around her neck, even when she bathed, even when they made love.

So Jesse didn't know to be worried. Didn't know that his daughter was in danger. Couldn't even think about his daughter, in fact, while he was bearing the dead body of his wife on his shoulder. Each slow step sucked his feet deeper into the mud. He was being buried too.

He pretended that he wasn't there. That she wasn't there in the box. That was the only way he could do it. To shut his eyes to the damp, dark forest. To shut his ears to the sounds of Stewey stumbling on behind him, wheezing quietly as he wept. To shut his heart to the sight of his own little girl hitting the box with her fist and crying out words he could not understand.

He shut his eyes and pretended he was walking to the well. He was walking behind that pretty little gal in blue who swung her hips for him and spilled water on his boots when she handed him the dipper. He was running behind her in the tall grass and catching at her knees and pulling her down and laughing, she kept laughing, when he covered her lips with his, and she lifted her soft arms to him and wouldn't let him up. He was carrying her boots for her when she plunged into the creek and rolled in the icy water and then lay out in the sunlight like some kind of a mermaid from a picture book, with her hair slicked back from her shining face and her dress clinging tight as scales to her round breasts, her belly, her hips, wrapping itself down to a point, just like she didn't have any feet at all.

Jesse had always been standing behind her. Never could catch up. And that was just fine with him. All of a sudden, that was just right. Just to stand behind and watch her move. And carry her boots.

Jesse's eyes were so filled with India that he didn't see Singing Bird at all. Didn't see her darting between trees, following his daughter with her eyes, grabbing at the little girl's sleeve with her long, blackened fingers.

But Greta did. She saw her. She rode up just in time.

Greta learned about India from Brewster Ruggles. She'd walked in on him one day at Salkeld's. She'd found him stacking and unstacking bolts of fabric, muttering something that she couldn't understand. When she asked what was ailing him, he handed her the telegram. Jesse sent it. Old Salkeld was laid up with rheumatism so Ruggles was obliged to help out at the store. Couldn't leave. Wanted to, but couldn't. His hands were shaking as he spoke. He piled the calico on top of the corduroy, on top of the yellow silk. Then he shook his head and started a new pile, reversing the order. "It's still not right," he said to himself. "I just can't get it right."

Greta booked passage on a boat named *Mystic*, then borrowed a horse in town and charged through the winding woods. White Cloud had taught her how to ride like that, with her thighs vised tight around the horse's ribs, with the reins loose and snapping in the morning air. Her back was strong. Her arms were strong. She leaned forward from her hips. She caught hold of Jessamyn's arms and lifted her up without breaking stride. She set the child before her on the great gray horse and told her not to be afraid.

The child said nothing. Just allowed herself to be carried away. She clung to the animal's mane with one hand only; the other she let float and fly in the feathery gray mist that encircled their heads and enveloped the forest. She looked back once to meet the gray eyes of her rescuer, but even then saw only the great wooden box that loomed before her and behind her and was filled with settled sadness.

Then she saw something else.

It was the Big Blue and the yellow sun all splashed together in one single drop. It was the red and gold blaze of a prairie fire pressed into one lick of flame. It called to her. It called like a purple berry warming on a gray-green vine.

"Stop!" the child said then, and Greta had to pull the reins up quick because the child was already wriggling off the horse and slipping to the earth.

The stone was alive again. It was shooting colors like stars into the dark morning. Jessamyn tore through the pile of dead leaves and captured the stone in her small muddy hands. She held it high, like a trophy, and laughed when it lit up the sky.

Jesse opened his eyes. His daughter was not with him. He asked Stewie, Brodie, Cam. He ran and ran. He saw something bright. He found her. He dropped to his knees, crushed her in his arms. "Where in the hell . . ." he started to scold, then turned to the woman in gray. "Who are you?" he said, without rising.

Jessamyn told him not to worry, that the woman was a friend of mama's, that she just saved her from the witch.

Greta knelt down beside them then and helped the child loop the chain over her head. The stone sparkled on the dull black linen of the cut-down mourning cloak. Jessamyn bounced up and down on her heels to make the stone prance across her chest.

"Where's the witch?" Jesse asked. He was smiling, gently, because his baby's laughter eased into his joints like liniment and he didn't want it to stop. He squinted hard and pretended to be searching for his daughter's imaginary pursuer. His youngest had always had quite an imagination. Just like her ma. He opened his eyes wide then and just let the tears burn as he studied his baby's bright hair, her bright eyes, the bright stone, the limp, muddy socks that swam around her bony ankles. He might have lost her too.

"Over there," Jessamyn said, pointing at the sycamores. She was too busy playing, just then, with the silvery sparks that leapt from her stone to her fingers to care about witches, but both Greta and Jesse saw the old woman with the long white braids, the long black fingers, the dangling smile.

Jesse sprung up quick to shield his daughter. Greta lifted her hand in greeting. Singing Bird raised her blackened palm then turned, slowly, without moving her feet. She glided deeper and deeper into the shadowy forest until they couldn't see her anymore. Her coral bracelets made a small, fragile music in the darkness.